The Lobster's State of Mind

By : Hovav Heth

D1004750

2

Contents

The Lobster's State of Mind

Sharon looked around Daniel's room. On the table by the computer there was a pile of articles he was reading for his seminar paper and a few printed pages lying on top of them. There was a book by Hanif Kureishi with a bookmark in it and a Cyprus guidebook he had bought for the trip they had been planning for the end of the semester. Everything seemed like yesterday, as it had always been, as if her world hadn't shattered. The sheets lay on the bed practically as if Daniel had just gone to the bathroom for a minute, a hollow in the pillow where his head had rested, the blanket casually thrown back, and she could still smell the body that had been lying there two days ago – it all seemed so unreal. Something caught her eye; there was something small stuck between the bed and the wall. She climbed on to the bed where she had spent so many nights and then froze: she was erasing the shape of his body and his smell in the sheets. She tried to pick up whatever it was without messing up the bed too much. It was a little pill, a half-red, half-white capsule. This was very strange. Sharon felt around with her fingers where the pill had been and found another one. What was that supposed to mean? Now she was angry and frantic rather than prudent. She got off the bed, grabbed it with both hands, pulled it away from the wall, and immediately heard the sound of many small objects falling on the floor. What the hell was that? Sharon tried to understand, and she thought how weird it was that only a week before, they had celebrated her twenty-third birthday.

The waiter poured some wine into Daniel's glass and stood beside him, bottle in hand, waiting for Daniel's verdict. Daniel, who was quite ignorant in such matters, smiled, picked up the glass and sniffed it like a real wine connoisseur:

"Mmmm, a hint of almond bloom... a ripe guava... some laundry powder, very expensive powder, maybe some softener as well..."

Sharon giggled, "You're so funny!"

"Then why are you laughing if I am soooooo funny?"

"I'm being polite."

Daniel stuck his tongue out in her direction, then he bent across the table for a kiss. The waiter stood patiently with the bottle in his hand.

"I'm sorry, do pour us some wine, please."

"That's quite all right. Have you decided what to order or would you like a few more minutes?"

"We're OK. I'll take the lobster in white wine and garlic, and Sharon?"

"You're eating lobster? Well done! I'll take the sea food casserole with cream sauce and mushrooms."

Daniel had always been too cautious where food was concerned. He raised his glass: "To our love, until we're a hundred and twenty!"

"Oh." Sharon grabbed him by the back of the neck and gave him a big kiss on the mouth. Daniel emitted rather a loud sigh.

"My God, everybody is staring at us," she whispered, and as if to confirm this observation, a middle-aged woman smiled at them and raised her glass: "Look at them dear, they're such a cute couple!"

Daniel smiled at her and raised his glass.

"I need to go to the bathroom. I'll be right back."

He went toward the corridor leading to the toilet, passed by a half-open door and peeked in. Lots of pots and pans lined the wall and there was a strong smell of frying and spices. A chef showed up with a lobster in his hands, helplessly moving its jointed legs around. The free claws seemed quite menacing, but the experienced chef seemed very calm and definitely unharmed. Daniel opened the door slightly and went inside. Could this be the unfortunate one he was about to consume? It couldn't be; his order hadn't even reached the kitchen yet. This was probably someone else's unfortunate lobster.

On the other side of the kitchen, another chef armed with a big knife was chopping onions with incredible dexterity.

"Excuse me. May I be of any assistance?" The chef had a slight French accent and he seemed very friendly.

"I'm sorry, I was just a little curious. I'm out of here."

"No, no, it's perfectly OK."

"It's just that I'm about to eat my first lobster and I saw you with this lobster, so… that's it."

"It's OK. Look, first we cook it in hot water and then we shall bake it. You see this big pot?" the French chef lifted the lobster over the pot.

"Are you cooking it alive? Why don't you kill it first?"

"Oh no, but they die quite quickly, there is no problem."

He put the lobster in the pot and a terrible whistling sound emerged. Daniel felt his stomach turning inside out.

"Was that the water?"

"No, it's the lobster," said the pleasant chef, smiling. "I think this might have been a bad idea, huh? Oh well, we learn from experience. I am so used to this and… I am really sorry, I hope you will forgive me."

"Oh no, it's my fault, I came into this place uninvited. Thank you very much for your kindness."

Daniel's stomach continued to feel funny and he quickly got out of the kitchen and hurried back to the table. "Oh, gross! I want to change my order."

"What happened, was it dirty in the bathroom?"

"No, I forgot to go to the bathroom. Do you know what they're doing in the kitchen? They're boiling the lobster while it's still alive! That's terrible!"

Sharon laughed. "Oh dear, didn't you know that's how they make them? You're so ignorant!" But she caressed his hand and added empathetically: "You had a little shock, do you want Mummy to comfort you?"

"Oh, it's so cruel! Who wants to eat a lobster after it's been boiled to death?"

"What difference does it make? It's just a lobster."

"It's a living thing, isn't it? I bet it doesn't want to be cooked alive any more than I do." "That's nonsense! The lobster doesn't want anything. Lobsters have no self-awareness, no concept of self; it makes no difference if you keep them alive, fry them or hang them."

"How can you be so sure? Why should a lobster have no self-awareness if a mosquito does? When I try to kill a mosquito, it makes very serious efforts to avoid being killed. They certainly act like they really want to live!"

"Any living organism has survival skills; it doesn't turn them into self-aware creatures. Take for example a huge school of fish. Studies conducted on them have shown that a single fish doesn't show any signs of individual behavior, nothing that differentiates it from the other fish.

Those little fish and the lobster as well are automatic survival mechanisms, like politicians. They just live to produce another generation."

"Ha, ha, now you're funny!"

"It doesn't matter if I'm funny or not. Saying that the lobster wants or the lobster is scared is completely meaningless. If you are not aware, you have no desires, so there is no moral difference between throwing a living lobster into boiling water or doing the same to an alarm clock, only the lobster is tastier."

"I'm not so sure you're right. It seems to me kind of presumptuous to determine with such confidence whether they are self-aware or not. You can't even be sure if I am aware. You can only be sure about yourself, so how can you be so sure about the lobster?"

"Don't get so philosophical. There are indications that tell me that the alarm clock is an inanimate object, that the lobster is an unaware living organism, and that you – well, to be quite honest, you're right: I'm not so sure about you."

Sharon laughed loudly.

"I'm very happy to see you so amused by yourself, but I'm going to change my order. I'm going to eat the salmon fillet."

"Ah, I knew that eventually we'd end up with salmon. I must warn you, though, I don't think the salmon had such a swell time getting here!"

"Well, at least it got here dead so I don't have to watch it being tortured!"

After dinner, Daniel took Sharon to her parents' house. It was an old Jerusalem-stone house in the German Colony with arched windows and blue wooden shutters, and around it was a beautiful, well-kept garden.

"Why do you have to pick up your parents from the airport today of all days?"

"It only means that the presents will be much nicer!"

"Oh well, I can wait in your apartment, that's no big deal."

"I don't think I'll get there tonight. Do you forgive me? I'll make it up to you tomorrow. It's just that the unpacking and opening of the presents stage is very long with my parents, and it'll probably end early in the morning. Anyway, in a month, there will be no more 'your place' and 'my place' – there'll only be 'our place'!"

Sharon went to the bathroom, and Daniel walked around the house and went out on to the circular back terrace that overlooked the garden. There was a wonderful fragrance in the air. Against the wall stood a heavy reddish closet that seemed to be a hundred years old, like most of the stuff in the apartment, but while most of the furniture was in good condition, the closet seemed to be kind of disintegrating.

"Sharon!" he yelled. "What's this old closet on the terrace?"

"It's been here since my grandparents built the house, more or less. There's lots of old stuff inside it. I don't think anybody has opened it in the last fifty years."

Daniel opened the closet. Inside were piles of yellowish papers, old dusty folders and old books. He took a few papers – old drawings of animals – and at the bottom of one of them it said: "Amos Goldberg, 1953".

"My dad did these when he was a kid." Sharon was already standing next to him.

"I didn't know he had such talent, your dad."

Under the drawings was a pile of old magazines. Daniel took one out and tried to shake the dust off it.

"Wow, October 1943!" On the cover was a photograph of an American WWII fighter. "You have such amazing things here. We should really search this place – who knows what we'll find."

Daniel took out a little book that appeared to be red under a thick layer of dust. He opened it; it looked like some kind of a diary. The pages were covered with short lines in tiny handwriting. Some of the lines rhymed. "Is he a poet, your dad?"

"No, that's not his handwriting."

"Then who wrote this?"

"I have no idea! Since my grandparents built the place, many people have been here. How should I know?"

"Wasn't it weird for your dad to go back and live in the house he grew up in?"

"Maybe. After my grandparents moved to protected housing for the elderly, it was either selling it or having someone move in, and my dad really didn't want to sell, so we moved in."

Daniel leafed through until he got to a page whose corner was folded down and read:

The Lord, for all that he created
For all who dwell between the poles,
He tore away his own awareness
So he could give them equal soul

He didn't care for shape or size
For unlike man he was so wise
And thus all living creatures won
Those pieces of awareness torn

The human being, the little ant
He breast-fed with the milk of soul
A drop to this one, a drop to that
Their places equal in his heart

When wretched men with vicious feet
Tread down upon a nest of ants
The damage caused is so complete
Our lord can't stand the sight of it

The ants that die make horrid cries
Though human beings can't hear them crying
But for the Lord it's just as loud
As that of scores of people dying

"Wow!"
"Wow, what?"
"This is like an answer to our argument!"
"This is not an answer to anything; it's a nice poem, no more, no less.
When did you become such a mystic, anyway?"

"I don't know. Maybe I'm becoming a mystic right now! I mean, first we talked about whether animals are aware, and now, completely by chance, I find a book marked at the exact page where there is a poem about it. Doesn't it strike you as fate?"

"Oh dear, I hope we're not going to discuss fate now. I have to get going, you know? It's my fate to pick my parents up at the airport every time they fly."

"Why can't they take a cab?"

"That's not very nice; I might have to report it to my dad. Anyway, I like picking them up from the airport in the middle of the night." They kissed and said goodbye and Daniel went to his apartment.

Daniel opened the door to his building and looked in suspiciously. He inspected the corners of the entrance, the ceiling and the two big flowerpots. It wasn't dangerous burglars he was afraid to find, but cockroaches. For a few weeks now, there had been a terrible infestation of cockroaches. These weren't the ugly little one-centimeter creatures he used to find at his parents' place from time to time; the cockroaches in his building were mighty, scary insects. They were two inches or more in length and were covered with a brownish yellowish armor that contained a substantial meaty mass. Stepping on them caused a horrible cracking sound. Their long, rigid antennas moved nervously in all directions as they cruised around at a hundred miles an hour, and when Daniel spotted one of them around, he would always panic, fearing that the monster might attack him with those long ugly feelers. That had never happened, obviously, but Daniel was quite convinced that should it happen, he would have a heart attack and die on the spot.

Daniel stepped in and called the elevator. When it arrived, he opened the door and inspected its interior before entering. Wherever he had had a traumatic encounter, he would act this way. He opened the door to his apartment, turned on the light and looked around to make sure his apartment was clean. During the first few minutes in his home, he would always behave like an explorer walking through new and uncharted territory, inspecting the kitchen and bathroom before entering. Only after a few minutes, when he had regained his confidence, would he behave like a true proprietor.

He went into his bedroom, inspected it again, and when he was absolutely sure it was safe, put his rucksack on the chair, sat on his bed and stretched his muscles. What a pity Sharon couldn't be with him now. Together, everything was much easier. He thought about the seminar paper he had to submit. His topic was the big economic crisis in Japan, and he and his partner spent hours in the library searching for material. Everything they found seemed inadequate to their academic advisor. Every article was either too complicated for undergraduates to handle or too simple.

Daniel heard mincing sounds behind him and jumped frantically to his feet. Now, when he was finally at ease, the infiltrator appeared – from a very unexpected hideout: the warmth of his bed-linen. Daniel stood frozen and looked at the cockroach with horror. He was overwhelmed by panic, his knees began to tremble, practically paralyzing his legs as the cockroach cruised along the bed, descended to the floor, and then went into hiding in the little space under the closet between the drawers and the floor.

Daniel knew that he wouldn't be able to sleep before the monster lay dead before him. He went out of his room and into the kitchen, looking back from time to time to make sure the beast hadn't left its place under the closet, and returned armed with a weapon of mass destruction – a can of insecticide. He held the can upside-down, stood at a safe distance from the closet so he wouldn't get caught in the cockroach's escape route, and began spraying under the drawers like a madman, heedless of the fact that in an hour or so, he would have to sleep in the very same room. His whole body was covered with sweat, even though it was a cool Jerusalem night, and he felt quite stupid.

Daniel was very intelligent and some of his fears seemed to him quite important for his survival. He was scared to death of anything to do with motorcycles. He always refused his friend Roy's suggestions to join him for a ride on his Suzuki 500 – one mistake and they would both end up smashed against some concrete wall. This was a reasonable fear and Daniel felt no need to apologize for it. His irrational fears, however, caused him shame: Daniel could never bring himself to watch a horror movie with his eyes open; in the scary scenes, he would always look sideways or partially covered his eyes with his hands. This made him feel uncomfortable about himself; after all, whatever damage could the two-dimensional creatures on the screen cause him? But the fear of cockroaches was the worst, and with the recent infestation, it had become quite exhausting and even intolerable.

Daniel believed that in order to overcome his fears, he had to face and confront them. Using this rationale, he hoped that if he could bring himself to stamp on one of the horrid creatures, his fear of them would vanish. When he walked in the street, the encounter with the monsters was less traumatic. Sometimes when he ran into them, Daniel would stand near them (but not too close) and try to make that decisive move.

He would approach them, prepare his right leg for the final blow, hesitate, walk away, and come closer again, keeping the beast in his sights. He would sometimes find himself wasting precious minutes transfixed, reluctant to admit his defeat, but unable to step on the ugly insect. So he would stand there until he got the feeling that people were beginning to stare at him, and then he would walk away defeated.

Now Daniel stood in front of the closet waiting for the cockroach to reveal itself, but it didn't. Daniel began to worry that the beast had escaped while he was in the kitchen and was now waiting to ambush him somewhere else. He knocked cautiously on the closet with no effect. Finally, he took a squeegee and began moving it violently under the closet drawers. After a few seconds, the cockroach came out staggering like a drunk from the overdose of insecticide it had received. Daniel froze and then tried to hit the beast with the squeegee. He missed by a millimeter, but the cockroach turned over and lay helplessly on its back, twitching. Daniel was about one yard away from it: its rough-textured legs moved desperately back and forth, its ugly antennas moved left and right.

Daniel's heart was beating fast and a big drop of sweat dripped off his forehead and landed on the floor. Would he be able to master his fear, demonstrate his superiority over the little creature, and squeeze it to death? After about a minute of staring, Daniel found himself a lot more relaxed and feeling very foolish indeed. Here he was, six feet of muscle and stupidity trembling and sweating when facing a helpless little creature that weighed a lot less than his little finger. Why did he hate them so much, these pathetic little animals? Maybe, he thought, maybe this was the other side of the disgust he felt toward his own irrational fears, toward the part of him that felt small and stupid like the cockroach that was now dying in front of him.

Daniel suddenly remembered the poem he had read earlier that evening and the lobster he wouldn't eat. In what way was this cockroach any worse than ants and lobsters? Did it deserve this terrible fate just because nature had made it so unpleasant to the human eye? No, Daniel decided, and he felt conscience-stricken about the agony he was inflicting upon this miserable creature. If it was self-aware (Daniel was not quite sure about that), what did it feel now, this cockroach facing imminent death? Maybe it was scared or maybe it accepted its fate and was now waiting for the final blow that would put it out of its misery. These thoughts did not free Daniel from his feelings of disgust when he looked at the cockroach, but he gently turned it over with the squeegee. The cockroach wobbled some and it seemed like it wouldn't last very long. After a few yards of slow movement that led to the living room, it turned over on its back again. Should he leave it be in its final moments or put an end to its suffering? Daniel would never know the answer. He lifted his foot and stepped decisively on the creature, making sure that death was instantaneous. The cracking sound was quite atrocious. The cockroach was smeared over the floor with substantial remains on the sole of Daniel's shoe. He took lots of folded toilet paper, cleaned up the remains, and threw it into the toilet. Due to the short notice, it was impossible to prepare a proper funeral, he said smiling as he flushed.

Daniel went to sleep with some troubling questions in his mind: How many cockroaches had he killed? How many ants and mosquitoes? If all of these were conscious creatures, then he was a mass murderer.

Sharon stood by Daniel's door and knocked.

"Daniel, are you there? Answer me, you jerk!" For a few days he had been avoiding her, not returning calls, or saying he would talk to her the next day.

Could Daniel have found a new girlfriend? Now, after they decided to live together and after his declaration of eternal love? Daniel was lying in bed and felt awful. He wanted to see Sharon terribly, but he didn't want her to see him and the apartment in their present state. He needed some more time to try and explain himself and to tidy up the mess. Maybe when he was better he would make a little zoo for his new little friends. He heard the key turn – ah, what a fool, he forgot that she had a key to the apartment; he should have left his key in the keyhole. He jumped hurriedly out of bed and tried to figure out what to do, but it was definitely too late.

Sharon entered the apartment and looked at the living room; it took a few seconds before she realized what she was seeing. The big window was wide open and the cool Jerusalem wind was blowing in. In the center of the room stood a big garbage can overflowing with garbage. The smell was awful. Three ferocious-looking cockroaches were walking smugly on it. In the corner there was another smaller garbage can topped with fruit remains, and a variety of insects were standing there having the time of their lives. One evidently dead cockroach was lying on its back and a long line of ants stretched from it. Sharon screamed, then she cautiously entered Daniel's room, not knowing quite what to expect. Daniel was sitting on his bed looking quite dazed. Sharon sat by him, caressed his cheek and looked in his eyes, trying to determine what kind of a mental state he was in.

"Oh dear, you look awful. What's the matter with you? Have you lost it completely? Have you decided to open a zoo in here?"

"What? Oh, no, no."

"So what is that?"

"Well, it's… it's… Remember the conversation we had a few days ago?"

"Which conversation?"

"In the restaurant, when we talked about the lobster and whether animals are self-aware or not."

"Yeah?"

Sharon found it very difficult to understand what he was talking about and she felt like her head was about to explode. She looked at Daniel and suddenly felt as if she were looking at a complete stranger, as if she had woken up to an unfamiliar reality after hibernating for a few years. Who was this man she was talking to? She closed her eyes, took a deep breath and tried to relax and understand what he was saying to her.

"So I figured, if these guys are self-aware, why don't I do something for them? I'll clean this, I promise, I just have to regain my strength and then I'll move them somewhere. Ah, look at this monster!"

Daniel laughed as Sharon screamed. "I put up a 'Do not disturb' sign, but apparently they can't read."

Sharon stepped angrily on the cockroach.

"Why did you do that? That's exactly what I'm trying to avoid now." Sharon's head still hurt, but at least she had now figured out more or less what he was trying to say, and it didn't make her feel any better.

"My sweet, I think you kind of temporarily lost your mind, but I'm going to clean up this place and then we're going to see a doctor."

"Ah, nonsense, I just got the flu, that's all."

"Honey, you look like shit and I want you to see a doctor. Maybe we should go to the emergency room. Now, if you'll excuse me, I'm going to take care of your little friends; I really hope you'll forgive me."

"Don't kill them, you don't need to kill them, they want to live, too."

"Oh, shut up, will you?" she screamed, wanting to cry.

That was it! Could things ever go back to what they used to be? What had happened to this world, anyway?

"Sharon, I don't want you to kill them."

She quickly left the room and locked it.

"Sharon, I don't want you to kill them. You can just throw them out or something," he screamed, and banged on the door.

"I'll throw you out, you moron!" Sharon went to blow her nose and wipe the tears and she was relieved to have Daniel locked in his room. She began a thorough clean-up of the apartment, killing all the new tenants in spite of Daniel's angry screaming and banging on the door that lasted a few minutes until he got tired.

After a few minutes of work, she found that she was more relaxed and had regained her mental abilities, more or less. She tried to understand this bizarre change in Daniel; it was as if he had converted overnight to a new religion. Was it for always? Would he become a vegetarian and refrain from even killing mosquitoes for the rest of his life?

Perhaps the new ideology wasn't quite formulated. Would this mania go away in a few days? And what about them? Could she live with this man or was this the end? Sharon suddenly felt how terribly she missed Daniel, the old Daniel, and she went to his room and cautiously opened the door. Daniel lay in bed and looked at her with accusing eyes.

"Does it really bother you that I killed those ugly cockroaches and some ants and stuff?"

"Yeah!" he said, sounding like an insulted little boy. Sharon sat on the bed and felt his forehead.

"You have a serious fever. I'm calling the doctor, OK?"

"Do whatever you want."

Dr. Friedman had been her family's doctor for twenty years. He arrived an hour later, gave Daniel some antibiotics, and told Sharon to make sure Daniel took the entire course on time and to call him should things deteriorate. Over the following days, Sharon tried to spend as much time as possible with Daniel.

She brought some chicken soup prepared by her mother and made sure he took his medications on time. Daniel apologized for alarming her and admitted that he had behaved like a fool. For a few days it seemed to Sharon that he was regaining his strength and becoming his old self again.

And then, three days later, she got up to find him feverish, pale, mumbling incoherently and generally looking like he was about to die. It took him a few minutes to realize who she was. Sharon called an ambulance and Daniel was quickly taken to the emergency room and from there directly to the ICU.

His parents and two sisters arrived later from the north of Israel, and Sharon sat with them consumed by guilt. Obviously, she had talked to Orna, Daniel's mother, and told her he was sick – Daniel had spoken to his mother as well – but she had told her that things were under control and that there was no need for her to come all the way to Jerusalem. She hadn't shared this zoo madness with anyone, and now, as they sat facing the closed door of the ICU, not knowing what to expect, she wondered if she made the right choices. Why had she censored this information? She had thought how embarrassing this story would be for Daniel and that she shouldn't alarm his mother – what a fool she was! Orna might have realized earlier how dangerous things were. And why had Dr. Friedman's antibiotics failed to work? Why hadn't she just taken him to the hospital? How important she felt when she summoned the loyal family doctor and discussed the symptoms with him, especially when the possibility of using some prestigious and expensive medical institution was mentioned! Such stupid aristocratic arrogance. What use was all the family money and heritage if she didn't have a grain of common sense?

She hadn't shared the whole truth even with Dr. Friedman, He was a medical specialist, not a theologist, right? Still, why hadn't she shared this burden with someone?

After spending a grim evening together, they sat shifts: Mother and Dorin, who was 14, were first, then Dad and 17-year-old Alona, and Sharon took the last shift. In the morning, they all gathered near the ICU, but the doctors still wouldn't let them see Daniel. Finally, at one p.m., a sad-looking doctor came out to them and his miserable face was all they needed in order to know what he was about to tell them: Sharon started to cry and Dorin asked what that meant and then they all started to cry and the doctor said he was sorry. Now Sharon was standing by Daniel's bed and she realized that he hadn't taken the pills prescribed by the doctor. She herself had seen him put them in his mouth and had been convinced that he had swallowed them. Why had he deceived her like that? She moved the bed a little further from the wall and shook it some more and another pill fell to the floor.

She brought a broom and swept up all of the dirt under the bed, and then she collected the pills from the little pile of dust and arranged them in three rows on the table like a military formation. She opened the closet and took out the box of antibiotics. It contained thirteen pills. There was a total of forty-one pills on the table. The doctor had prescribed six pills a day for seven days. One pill was missing. Could he have swallowed one by mistake, or maybe she had missed one pill? She returned to the bed, took the pillow and blanket and shook them violently. Then she took off the sheet and shook the mattress. She gave the floor another sweep but didn't find anything. Why was she trying so hard anyway? As if by finding the missing pill she could bring Daniel back from the dead.

She remembered that Dr. Friedman had always stressed the importance of taking *all* the antibiotics. Maybe taking just a little made things even worse.

She went to the living room, sat on the couch and started to cry. Why did she deserve this trauma at the age of twenty-three? So far, her life had been so nice – a pretty girl from a good family, a true fairy tale, and now this! Why did she have to meet him? It was all because of that stupid lobster. Why did she try to change people? Who cares if a person doesn't eat seafood? Sharon looked at her watch. She had been sitting there for twenty minutes sobbing, feeling sorry for herself. Enough! She got up and looked around her and went back to the bedroom. She looked at the rows of pills on the table again. What was it that Daniel said before the ambulance arrived? Actually, those were their last moments together. In the ambulance the paramedic had worked on him, and she couldn't even hold his hand most of the drive. He said he was sorry and sighed and mumbled and Sharon cried and said there was nothing to be sorry about and then he said something else, something to do with the madness that began this whole thing.

"Do you think they're self-aware?" he said, and she asked, "Who, my darling?" He didn't answer and continued to sigh, but right before they got into the ambulance, when he was already in the wheelchair, he said: "The germs, I was talking about the germs." And now, with the antibiotics he hadn't taken lying before her, she realized what he was saying: "Do you think they're self-aware, the germs?"

The Eulogy

"Would you like me to give you a blow job?"

The woman bent over his dick, her smelly feet by his head, her wrinkled thigh before him.

"Yeah, yeah, uh… yeah, that would be nice."

Having finished the sentence, David managed to remember her name and felt ashamed of himself. Jasmin, her name was Jasmin. When she descended toward his dick, her breasts swayed above him like drops of wax about to fall off their candle – so terribly flabby. Her nipples seemed like squashed cherries on a twig and David wandered if he really wanted this unattractive woman to coat his dick with her saliva. But he did nothing, partially because he didn't know what he wanted (stopping now would probably not allow him to honestly register her among his private statistics regarding his sex life in recent years – very poor statistics indeed), partially because he didn't want to hurt her, or maybe because inertia had taken over. In any case, he just lay there passively, allowing her to do as she wished.

He had met her in a bar in Haifa's Carmel Center: it was an old bar, pleasantly decorated, the walls covered from top to bottom with oil paintings, the work of Misha, the owner. David had met him when they were both in their twenties and David was a rising power in Israeli music. In recent years, he had been coming here twice a week, sitting at the bar and reminiscing about the old days with Misha: the big concert David had given in 1978 on Israel's thirtieth Independence Day and their childhood memories from the kibbutz. Most of the clients were at least fifty years old, people who knew and appreciated David. Many of them would pat him warmly on the shoulder or shake his hand.

There was nowhere else on earth where he received so much warmth and affection, and it almost made him feel important.

When Jasmin entered the bar and noticed David's presence in the establishment, she was truly excited. Misha, who understood the grandeur of the event, served her a Caramel Mist – an expensive creamy cocktail – on the house and told her that whoever drank with David always received VIP treatment in his bar. In the smoky darkness of the bar, Jasmin seemed tall and attractive. Only when they arrived at his place did he notice that five foot eight inches (David's height), more than four inches were attributable to her very high-heeled shoes. The long and elegant coat she wore throughout the evening until they reached his place concealed a disproportionate figure. When she approached him and sat next to him at the bar, David imagined seeing the coat curving along the lines of a round and juicy bottom. Now he discovered that not only was her bottom as flat as a board, but her body seemed to completely lack that graceful bottle-like figure that usually characterizes members of the female sex. Her face, which must have been pretty some years ago, looked a bit disfigured, probably due to residual scars from some skin affliction cured long ago, and she had a substantial boil right at the right corner of her mouth. When her lips drew closer to his dick, David dreaded a possible eruption that would leave his genitals covered with pus. Having finished the uninspiring sexual act, they lay side by side in silence, and David's greatest desire was that Jasmin would vanish, preferably completely disappear from this universe. He peeked sideways and saw her peculiar body lying there next to his. Her snores suddenly penetrated his awareness and he seemed to detect a strange smell from her side of the bed, similar perhaps to the smell of egg salad. He carefully rose from the bed and went to the bathroom.

After drinking some water, he stood in front of the mirror and took a long, hard look at himself: short, narrow drooping shoulders, a soft protruding belly hanging out of his underwear like an overflowing cake. No wonder the only woman he could sleep with was a fifty-two-year-old – two years older than him – who looked almost sexy, but only in total darkness.

Twenty years ago he had real groupies, young, sexy – but who was he trying to fool but himself? He never had an ounce of sex appeal. That had always been his problem; that's why the older Shalom Hanoch (A singer-famous in Israel) was still at the top of the charts while he was already long forgotten. He had always been too short, too small, too eager and lacking in self-confidence. Even in his days as a sweeping success, the girls didn't line up for him, and if he managed to get a good catch, she would always disappear after one miserable, awkward night.

Ten years ago, he had given his last concert at the kibbutz where he grew up, an event that still tormented and haunted him. At the time, he was still receiving substantial income from royalties, which, even now, were the source of a few shekels here and there, especially from songs he had written for other singers. He had two apartments he had inherited from his grandmother; he lived in the one on Moriah Street in the Carmel Center and rented the other one out. He managed to scrape a few jobs here and there: he had made a nice profit from writing the music for a children's play recently, and the play's success had given rise to hopes for more orders from that quarter, but that wasn't what he really wanted. David missed the days when his songs were at the top of the charts.

Nowadays his songs were only played in times of horrific terror attacks or on national memorial days, and even on this front he was losing ground; the music editors were becoming more and more liberal in their attitude toward days of mourning.

One evening not so long ago, he was making his way to Tel Aviv to visit an old friend. The radio was tuned to the army channel and David was listening to a DJ who presumed to be a sort of a fringe elitist. David was particularly satisfied when a listener asked to hear the song, *Martha's Harbor*, by the group All about Eve, one of David's all-time favorites. There you go, he thought. In spite of all the talk about a generation gap, good taste never loses its allure for some people at least. David's big comeback dreams resurfaced from the deep as they occasionally did – perhaps an album à la All about Eve? Alas, the smart ass of a DJ, who had annoyed David from the first second he heard his voice, informed the listener that the record had been destroyed and that a disc had not yet been purchased. He continued with a theatrical apology followed by a hysterical pledge to purchase the album as soon as possible.

"Then perhaps you can play *Oh My Precious Native Land* by David Ben Hillel?" In the first split second following this request, David was choked with excitement and he almost wept.

"Sure," the DJ said. "First we put on this masterpiece and then I play the fucking national anthem," and he started laughing as if he has just uttered a brilliant witticism and continued with a ridiculous imitation of David singing the beautiful song. David had felt so bad he decided to forgo the trip to Tel Aviv. He had called his friend and told him that his mother had fallen ill and the visit would have to be postponed. David tried to make up his mind whether to return to his bed or sleep on the living-room sofa.

The more the minutes passed, the uglier Jasmin seemed in his imagination, and the idea of going back and lying beside her seemed less and less desirable. On the other hand, was it not he who had brought her to his apartment? Nobody forced him to do that. He should assume responsibility for his actions.

If she were to wake up and discover that she had been abandoned in the middle of the night, she would probably feel terrible about herself, and David didn't want to do that to people, since he knew all too well what it was like to feel bad about oneself. David was a very nice person – too nice if he came to think of it – but that's what he was and there was nothing he could do about it. He stepped quietly into his bedroom and lay down beside her with extreme caution. After a few minutes that seemed like hours, and after turning over countless times, David realized that he wasn't about to get much sleep. Jasmin revived all his frustrations: how nice it would be to turn on the radio and stumble by chance upon one of his classics. Maybe when he died he would finally be accorded the honor he deserved. He would probably even commit suicide just for that purpose, but what was the good of eulogies he would never hear?

As these thoughts were passing through his mind, David was suddenly gripped with excitement as a new idea formed in his mind: he would do something completely outrageous, something no one had ever done before; but what was he going to do?

Would he kill himself? Certainly not! David would stage a fake death for himself and thus regain the taste of long-forgotten glory. And what then? He wouldn't want to pretend to be dead forever – he'd like to enjoy the fruits of his brilliant trick. Should he come out with a new album? Yes! Perhaps cover versions of his oldies but goldies or maybe brand-new material. Quiet love ballades! David had thousands of tunes in his head, waiting for the right moment, but nobody wanted to invest in him anymore and he feared the financial risks of an independent production. Perhaps a combination of old and new stuff? Anyway, he had enough time to figure it out.

David was so excited he couldn't stay in his bed for another second and he even forgot the need to keep quiet so as not to wake Jasmin. Having gotten up, he realized how much noise he had made.

Jasmin was looking at him half-asleep, and he shushed her as if reminding her to keep quiet and not wake the ones who were sleeping. He turned on the kitchen light and felt hungry and energetic. He set out a plate of nuts and seeds, poured himself a glass of whisky with dolphin-shaped ice cubes, and started drinking and nibbling. How wonderful it would be to hear the most powerful people in Israel expressing their grief at the death of the singer whose songs were synonymous with the Land of Israel. How could anyone even imagine the late sixties and the seventies without his music to give the people consolation? Enough! He should stop dreaming and be practical. How would he organize his fake death? He needed a body! A body ? Had he completely lost his freaking mind? David burst into liberating laughter. He should convince the world of his death without a body! And how would he do that? Maybe he should disappear and plant a suicide note where it would definitely be found. This plan had two major drawbacks:

1. David was not at all sure that a letter unaccompanied by a corpse would actually convince the world that he really was dead.

2. David was not sure that a suicide would be followed by such inspiring eulogies. People might speculate that his waning career was the reason for this desperate act. They might even mention that last performance.

David was appalled! He should organize a heroic death for himself. But how could he do that without a body? He ate two more roasted almonds and took a sip of his whisky. He would die oversees! Raul was the solution! Raul was a childhood friend of his.

His parents had emigrated from Argentina when he was five and they had grown up together on the kibbutz.

After his military service, Raul had gone backpacking in his native land and had never came back to Israel. Now he was living in some little town in Mexico and they still kept in touch.

David would go visit Raul in Mexico and together they would figure out how to carry out this plot. Raul had always been a naughty boy and his parents had to practically go down on their knees in order to convince Buki, the head of the kibbutz, to refrain from filing a complaint with the police after Raul burned down the barn. Yes, Raul would love to take part in this plot.

A week later, David landed in Cancun, Mexico. He spent one night in the cheapest hotel he could find in the famous resort city. The next day, he set off on the sixteen-hour journey along hundreds of kilometers of winding road that ascended to an altitude of over two kilometers to reach the town with the glorious name, San Cristobal de las Casas, where his childhood friend had chosen to settle. They had last seen each other more than five years ago during Raul's last visit to Israel. Raul was waiting for him at the San Cristobal bus station, and the two old friends hugged for a

long while as David struggled to contain the tears that flowed
uncontrollably. Raul's girlfriend, a beautiful thirty-year-old mestiza
called María, laughed and said in a charming Mexican accent:

"I see that I am no longer needed here." Raul made the introductions.
María kissed David on the cheek, and he felt this confusing mixture of
wonderful human warmth and great frustration – here again he was
reminded of how much he lacked that thing that God, with such cruel
generosity, had given Shalom Hanoch and his friend Raul.

Having calmed down a bit, David looked around him and was initially
depressed by the poor condition of the bus station. The dark sky seemed
menacing as well: for most of his trip from Cancun, a horrendous
downpour had pounded ceaselessly on the bus, and David,

sitting in the front seat, had watched with horror as the wipers struggled
heroically to clear the water off the windscreen.

But after getting into Raul's old VW Beetle cabriolet and riding through
town for a few minutes, David decided that he had probably landed
unintentionally in heaven. The air was cold and clear; David took a deep
breath and thought that he had never tasted air that was so tasty and
crispy. They drove through the little streets among rows of colorful
houses – blue houses, brown houses, yellow houses – and they all seemed
to have been painted the day before, all wonderful and aesthetic. They
stopped for a walk in the main square, crowded with people walking
about and filling the cafés and restaurants. The square was surrounded by
beautiful colonial buildings, and one side of it was completely occupied
by a big cathedral. David gave Raul an inquisitive look:

"She… is she a…?"

"María? But of course, she's a kosher Jewish girl, what else? A Mexican girl who spent all her life in the Chiapas and is called María, what do you say about that, huh? David, I love you and you haven't changed one bit."

"And that doesn't bother you?"

"Listen, do you remember that time when Buki wanted to kill me after I burned down the barn?"

"Sure, that's not the sort of thing one tends to forget."

"Right. Anyway, believe it or not, then, when I was only twelve years old, I learned an important lesson. I don't know if it was necessary to burn down a barn for that, but I guess that's what it took in my difficult case. After the fire, after my father slapped me so hard my head almost fell off..."

"Your accent is getting much worse."

"You're right, and I'm a little saddened by this development. As I was saying, after my father nearly put me out of business, he told me:

'You should know, Raul, that you are very lucky because a barn is nothing at all. But if you had killed someone today, it wouldn't matter if you were put in prison or if we managed to keep you out of jail – you would never forgive yourself because if you take someone's life, you take something you can never give back.' This taught me two important lessons that are actually one: that in life there is important stuff and there is bullshit, and María being a Catholic belongs to the bullshit department, and the second thing is that you only live once. We are not cats with nine lives, are we?

This one life should be lived to the full, and it doesn't matter if Mother is angry about my Catholic girlfriend. I can tell you this, next year we're going to get married and have babies and I will never leave this place."

"It's really so beautiful here."

"Exactly! Think of it this way: if God decided to create heaven in Mexico and decided to put a cathedral smack in the middle of it, then maybe it's not such an awful sin to marry a Catholic girl. What do you say about that?"

They rode to Raul's house on the outskirts of town, a modest house with two floors, a blue roof and a nice little garden. María prepared a delicious Mexican lunch and David and Raul talked about old times in Hebrew with Raul occasionally translating the highlights into Spanish. They downed lots of guacamole and tortillas piled with chicken and meat and vegetable dishes all seasoned with hot chili sauce that made David sweat, but he enjoyed every bite. Having finished the meal, they moved to the living room, sat back and stretched their legs, and Raul said:

"Shall we talk business?"

"Yeah. Is she...?"

"I tell María about everything that happens with me and you have nothing to worry about. She's quite sure that we're both crazy and she's probably right. Are you sure you want to do this?

After everybody finishes paying compliments to your dead body, do you really believe that this will help you get back in business?"

"I hope so, but I'm not sure. Look, I'm already here and I'm not going to back down now. I'm going all the way!"

"Not all the way, surely, huh? Anyway, maybe it's a good idea for you to do some crazy stuff; you've always been too nice and good."

The plan conceived by Raul and David was based mainly upon the intricate network of connections woven by Raul throughout the years. Eighty miles west and one mile below San Cristobal, there is a huge canyon walled by half a mile high rocks on both sides known as Canyon del Sumidero. In the canyon flows a river that terminates abruptly in a dam, creating a 300-yard-deep lake, deep enough to conceal David's body forever, and, of course, the alligators that abound in the lake would also supply an adequate solution to that problem. The Israeli embassy would report that an Israeli citizen whose name was David Ben Hillel had drowned in the river, having sacrificed his life to save the lives of two Indian boys who fell off the tour boat. After managing to pull them to the boat, the unfortunate David disappeared, never to be seen again. A few days later, while a grieving nation deplored the loss of the gifted artist, David would miraculously be found on the riverbank and would tell his amazing story to an excited nation. Raul knew a boat owner and two kids who would confirm the story for a certain sum, cops who were willing to report having found the missing singer after a few days, and a medical facility in which to hospitalize him for a period of recuperation. Raul needed a few days to organize the plot and David used those days to tour the town and make plans for his upcoming imaginary death.

The big day arrived. At six p.m., the embassy was informed of the tragic death of the renowned musician and poet, David Ben Hillel.

Six p.m. in Mexico was the middle of the night in Israel; it would take at least a few hours for the news to be reported in the Israeli media, and that suited David perfectly. At eleven p.m., Raul and María retired to their room on the second floor. David turned on the shortwave receiver that had been purchased especially for this event. He turned the volume high enough so that he wouldn't hear Raul and María making love, which practically drove him insane, but not too loud to disturb their sleep. At his request, María had prepared a selection of snacks to help him get through the night, and he spread them across the dining table. There was a plate of bean paste with crispy and oily Mexican chip snacks stuck in it, a big tortilla topped with ham and a fried egg and cheese and peas and delicious tomato sauce, a bowl of guacamole, a small plate of red chili sauce, a big pile of tortillas on another plate, two fresh yeast cakes, and a bottle of red wine purchased by David to help him withstand any crises he might encounter during the night. Tomorrow I start a strict diet, as soon as I'm dead, David said aloud, and managed to make himself laugh. He poured himself a glass of wine and decided to eat the egg dish.

When he had finished eating the first course, he felt a certain heaviness and regretted this uncalculated start to this crucial night. He felt like taking a short walk outside in order to facilitate the digestion of the food he had just consumed, but he decided to resist the temptation, as he had no batteries for his radio. Instead, he walked back and forth inside the living room, thus setting the pattern he would follow during the night: he ate, drank, walked around restlessly and then ate again. On the table by the food lay an Amos Oz novel that he hoped to finish during the sleepless night, but he obviously failed to read even a single page. He was far too nervous, and having made an attempt to read, which ended after three lines at the most, he decided to give it up.

After two hours of eating, David absolutely had to go to the bathroom, but what if he missed the crucial announcement? He managed to stretch the cable and place the radio just around the corner, some three yards from the bathroom door, and he sat there with the door open, praying that María wouldn't show up. After two minutes in the toilet, David heard a voice. He raised his head to find a beautiful woman standing next to him, staring at him. María? No, this woman had long, wavy brown hair as opposed to María's straight, shining black hair. She stood there in her high-heeled shoes, her slender figure wrapped in a long, elegant black dress. David looked at her pretty face, which was covered with red boils of various sizes, some of which exuded a yellowish liquid and seemed on the verge of erupting.

David jumped up in panic and his bottom slammed against the toilet seat. He found it hard to remember where he was. He heard strange voices talking to him; had he gone mad? A few seconds passed until David realized that the voices were coming from the radio at the end of the corridor and he regained his orientation. How long had he been sleeping in the toilet? He tried to understand the radio announcer and thought that his case was being discussed. He took a huge lump of toilet paper and gave his bottom an emergency wipe. He then leaped over to the radio with his trousers still down and his bottom exposed. A military analyst was discussing a possible outbreak of hostilities on the Lebanese border, and David went back to the toilet to finish his business there.

By five a.m., he was exhausted, and he considered giving up and going to sleep. Could something have gone wrong? Maybe Raul hadn't paid enough to the police officer who was to report his disappearance. He imagined Raul saying to him the following day:

"You should take the first bus to Mexico City, go to the Israeli embassy and refuse to leave until the ambassador is absolutely convinced you're dead!" Ha, ha, ha. Very funny. David strained his ears to be sure that he was indeed hearing the sounds that seemed to invade his sleepiness. Yes, there was no doubt. Ohhhh! sighed María, and in a split second, the drowsiness gave way to a kind of a horny nervous state. David got up from the sofa and went toward the staircase where he thought he might hear more sounds from the paradise on the second floor. Ahhhh! María added, and David could hear the bedsprings creaking in a perfect rhythm. Oyyyy! David had never made a woman utter such sounds. He sadly recalled the apathy he had demonstrated during his last sexual encounter. A few kisses and David lay down, mainly to escape the horrible boil near her mouth. Then she gave him a rather disappointing blow job and that was the end of it. He should have fucked her brains out! True, Jasmin was not the most desirable of women and yet she was a woman, she was there, waiting to be satisfied by him, the first woman he had conquered in almost a year – and he'd missed his chance. If he had been able to satisfy her, maybe that would have helped him regain his lost sexual confidence (although there hadn't been much to begin with). Oy! Oy! María burst into a series of loud sighs and David noticed that his right hand was buried deep in his pants, holding his erect penis. He was dying to go in the bathroom and jerk off this insufferable tension, but he was embarrassed; they might hear him. He went back to the sofa hoping to escape the passionate sighs, but they were audible everywhere, in the toilet, in the kitchen. Ohhhhh, sí!

David quickly walked toward the door and exited carefully, making sure not to slam it. He suddenly remembered that he had left the radio on; he might miss the important news. Uh, such nonsense!

He walked the streets tired and desperate. My life is hardly worth living, he thought. He had always believed that his songs were a way to attain immortality – in a hundred years, people would still derive consolation from his songs at a time when his richer friends`s stock portfolios would be long gone. Now, only twenty-five years later, most of his music had been thrown into the garbage can of history and his life was as miserable as his songs – no wife, no kids, and he didn't even live a proper single life. When was the last time he had enjoyed having sex? In fact, he tried to remember if he had ever enjoyed sex. Sex had been an ongoing frustration since he lost his virginity at nineteen in the military music troupe. And he didn't enjoy anything else, either. David suddenly realized that it had been a long time since he last felt truly alive; he was just passing time in a more or less bearable fashion. Maybe if he went to that big gorge and threw himself into the river and felt the alligator sink its teeth into his flesh – maybe then, for a few last seconds, he'd feel alive. David had lost his sense of time when he reached a hill on which stood a cathedral. He walked up the stairs until he reached the level of the cathedral. He remembered it to be a delicate azure in color, but in the pre-dawn darkness it was a big black mass. Fifty meters away there was a scenic lookout toward San Cristobal overlooking a thirty-yard cliff. It was ideal; the fall would kill him instantly. David held on to the railing and looked at the shadows of houses taking shape with the first rays of light. He took a deep breath and felt a tear slowly running down his cheek. Whenever he felt humiliated, the memory of that terrible last performance would haunt him.

A whole month before the big concert, posters were put up, announcing the return of the successful former kibbutznik to his home kibbutz.

David thought that he looked much better in the poster than in real life and it made him very nervous, as if he expected the audience to walk out on him or even boo him as soon as they discovered the truth.

This was supposed to be the first of a series of concerts titled "An Intimate Evening with David Ben Hillel" – David solo accompanying himself on the guitar or the piano. His previous tour, which had included a band of five and a chorus of three women, had been a failure and had caused him considerable financial damage. David hoped that a successful first concert on his native kibbutz would win over the critics and give him the right start for a good tour.

The concert began quite nicely. The kibbutz dining room was overcrowded with practically all the kibbutz members including many teenagers, and David felt almost like he had in the good old days. Lee, the kibbutz general secretary, made a warm speech, and when she finished she kissed him and gave him a very serious pinch on the cheek followed by loud cheers and a burst of warm laughter from the crowd. David sat on his high stool and as he tuned his guitar, he said: "What a great feeling to be home." A perfectly sensible phrase for a homecoming, but as he pronounced these words, David sensed a ring of artificiality to them. Ten years earlier he would have said those words with utter conviction, but now his career was going downhill, and David sounded rather pathetic and tired to his own ears and that embarrassed him. During the entire concert, David played and replayed this opening statement in his head, trying to find a tone suitable for such an optimistic sentence.

Suddenly, in the middle of the concert, David wasn't sure if this debate was going on within the confines of his own head or if he was talking to himself aloud, and that made him even more embarrassed. He looked at the countless heads arranged before him in rows and it reminded him of the Mediterranean waves he used to sit and watch for hours as a child. He would sit on the beach enchanted by the big blue sea and by the struggle between the waves storming the shore and the retreating waves, a struggle that yielded magnificent formations in the raging foam. "The sea waves," he said loudly, and then shook his head trying to free himself from the trance that he had fallen into as the crowd watched him in wonder. Alas, the sea waves began to move in the wrong direction: somewhere in the rear of the dining room, David noticed a few heads making their way out of the sea toward the exit. This was a group of youngsters that David didn't recognize and their leaving was certainly no major event. David was not the first artist to lose a few people during a concert and it wouldn't have turned into such an embarrassment if it hadn't been for David's insistence on marking the event. He felt an urgent need to protest against this wrongdoing, even though he knew it to be a terrible mistake. His following remark itched like a mosquito bite you know you shouldn't scratch and yet you can't resist. "Ah, I can see that a few youngsters are leaving us. Never mind, we are still here, singing our beloved old songs." How pathetic! The memory of this moment still tormented him; there wasn't another moment in his life that made him detest himself so much and feel such utter hatred for the crowd. This memory was usually accompanied by violent visions of the crowd perishing in a terrible fire or of him spraying the kibbutz members with a machine-gun. From that moment onwards, the trickle of people walking out became constant. He really shouldn't have been surprised; most of the deserters were teenagers who weren't even born when he wrote his big hits, but David felt as if his world has been shattered. His desperation was limitless and he continued to sing in a waning voice, his attention gradually drifting from the audience to his inner debate regarding the extent of the failure. He mentioned it almost every time someone walked out on him, and he embarrassed everyone when he said:

"Uh, I see Ron, Albert's eldest, leaving us. Isn't that a shame, Albert?"
By the end of the evening, there was still a very respectable crowd –

almost everyone over forty stayed with him – but he felt exhausted and he didn't want to give an encore. Encouraged by Lee, the crowd burst into wild applause and made him come back to the stage for two more songs, but he felt absolutely terrible. Later, as he walked the kibbutz paths alone in the night, he passed by a bunch of teenagers. One of them whispered: "Look at him, he looks like he's been run over by a heavy tractor," and his friends sniggered. The boy continued, probably not suspecting that his voice reached David's ears as clearly and sharply as a knife in the quiet night:

"He has some nice songs but what a terrible concert, an absolute disaster!" David continued to walk, pretending not to notice them, and he expected them to do the same, but he heard a voice calling him: "Sir? Goodnight, I mean it was OK, the show I mean..." followed by a burst of uncontrollable laughter. Until then, David had always felt like a teenager in the foreign land of adults, soon to be repatriated to the land of eternal youth. He had never felt so old. This was his last performance. All the other concerts scheduled for that tour were called off on the pretext of a health condition and he never went back on stage again. David looked down the cliff and it seemed as if he were looking into a bottomless well. At that moment, he realized that although leaping forward could have been a magnificent melodramatic ending to his life story, there wasn't a chance in the world that he would carry that out, perhaps because he was too scared and perhaps just because he wanted to live. He remembered the words of Raul about life and he suddenly thought that he should make use of his remaining years and stop worrying about what other people thought of him.

This foreign beautiful place could be the perfect spot for him because here, he really didn't care what others thought of him, except for Raul and María, and they had a great opinion of him.

He returned to their home to find them tired and worried. They had already alerted the police. David explained that he had gone out for a long walk because he couldn't sleep and he repeatedly apologized and enjoyed their affectionate scolds. That day, David and Raul listened together to a three-hour marathon held in his honor, featuring eulogies by Israel's best artists including Shalom Hanoch, who described him as an important composer and a moving singer and as the artist who linked the good old Israeli spirit with the seventies and eighties.

David and Raul decided to kill him off formally. The plan to hospitalize him after a miraculous rescue was abandoned. Raul used his shady contacts to get him a death certificate and some false documents and David learned Spanish, lived his life as Victor Hernandez, married Silvia, and made a living teaching the accordion in the Indian villages surrounding San Cristobal de Las Casas.

I am in a ditch, hiding. Above me is the watchtower, one of eight towers in the outer wall, four at the corners and one in the middle of each side. I can hear rockets being fired at me from the tower. I stealthily emerge from the water, make a small detour in order to reach the springboard from the correct angle, and a split second later I am already airborne, floating above the tower and seeing Claudius launching a multitude of rockets at another target. I am armed with my plasma blaster and I have Claudius right in the middle of my sights. I have but a few seconds until gravity draws me back to earth. I manage a few shots; at least one is a direct hit that should turn Claudius into a pile of grilled meat, but this bastard of a game cheats, I know that for a fact. I am playing the "Absolutely impossible" level and the moron programmers who invented this game didn't know how to make it more difficult in kosher ways, so they started cheating: you shoot accurately and hit nothing, and your enemies shoot poor shots that are right on the money, which is exactly what happens next. Claudius turns toward me; I am already making my way down to the inner grounds. He launches a rocket and I strife in time. That ought to save me for sure. But the same rocket that was making its way to my right is suddenly coming straight at me, leaving me no chance in the world of escape. My internal organs scatter all over the place as Claudius' voice mocks me:

"You piece of shit!"

I'm angry at Claudius and at the moron who invented this game and I wonder what kind of a fool I am to waste my time and energy getting angry at animated figures named after Roman emperors. I am a bitter person; I'm sure that everybody is out to get me, including Claudius and Tiberius. I have been playing this game for one year now, the same game and the same episode. I started when my girlfriend abandoned me to despair. During that tragic week about a year ago, I spent four to five hours every night playing this stupid game. In one week I managed to go all the way from "Truly unskillful" up to the respectable "Well, I guess you're OK" level. Now I'm playing the ninth level out of ten. When I started playing this game, I tried to play this level and lost in about two seconds: the idea that I would ever be able to play this level and give the emperors a decent fight seemed like a fantasy. I have improved tremendously since then – I haven't won this level yet, but it's a matter of time. I'm improving. The problem is that all the other aspects of my life are deteriorating. I seem to have exchanged my earthly life for the life of a virtual warrior. Take for example Merry, my ex-girlfriend and my motivator for slaying a hundred Roman emperors more or less every day and being slain by them a hundred and fifty times. We broke up a year ago and since then, nothing of any interest in that department has happened to me. A week after she left me, she reappeared in my house and raped me. That happened exactly one minute after my first victory at the "Well, I guess you're OK" level. She knocked on my door. I looked through the peephole, and when I saw her cute face, my heart leaped two yards up in the air and landed back in my chest. I couldn't believe my luck. I win my first grand victory at a challenging level and two seconds later, my dearest comes back to me like a Roman goddess welcoming a triumphant legionnaire! Alas, that was not to be.

I opened the door and my little dark Merry reached out and grabbed my balls. I hope you'll forgive me if I spare you the details. Suffice it to say, we had quite an orgy for two hours. I was a conqueror on two different fronts in a single night! And then, after lying side by side for five minutes, my precious got up. I was rather sleepy; after all, it was three a.m. and I had labored more than enough for one night. I continued to lie with my eyes closed, the lamplight penetrating my eyelids, waiting for the soft body of my love to cover me again. A few minutes later a voice addressed me:

"Danny?"

"Yeah?"

"I'm out of here."

"Where are you going?"

"Home."

"Wait a second." I sat up, barely awake.

"But... what?" I tried to formulate a question, but my brain was already deep in sleep mode. After a few seconds that seemed like eternity, I managed to say:

"But what does it mean?" Merry bent over me and gave me a motherly kiss on the forehead.

"It doesn't mean anything." And then she picked up her stuff and left, the bitch! I obviously couldn't sleep; my drowsiness was converted into the kind of nervousness that creeps into every cell in your body and doesn't allow you to stay put for a single second. I knew I'd have to find a way to get through the next two to three hours until exhaustion left me no choice but sleep. The solution was quite obvious. I sat by the computer, started

playing with a vengeance, and was sure that I would kick the asses of generations of Roman leadership again.

I was shamefully defeated. I was particularly angry at Augustus, whom I shot with a five-second burst of machine-gun fire right in the stomach, but the son of a bitch didn't want to die, or rather the asshole who created him didn't want him to die, and he turned to me and shot a shining blue plasma salvo that blew me off the face of the earth. I was angry.

I turned the computer off and called Romy. Romy works shifts and she is the only person I can call in the middle of the night. A week before, I could obviously call Merry. We met in our regular bar on Rothschild Boulevard. A week before, we had also met in the same place – Merry had just ditched me and Romy had given me valuable spiritual support. Romy is a beautiful and sexy woman. She looks far better than Merry, yet I have never felt any desire for her and it's quite obvious that she has never felt any for me. Actually, it's rather convenient and it makes me very proud. The thing is that we have been buddies since fourth grade and I can't think of her in a sexual way; it seems like incest. I picked her up at three thirty a.m., and by the time we got to the bar it was four a.m. There is something uplifting about being wide awake at four a.m., sitting in a bar on the sidewalk of Rothschild Boulevard, drinking beer and eating snacks. The air is far clearer and cleaner than at any other time and it makes you feel that you and the people around you belong to a special species that's still active at such a strange hour. And there's also the pain – the body seems to emit some kind of drug to help you deal with the pain. It makes you feel lucidly high in an odd way. Romy did her job – she was gentle and considerate, yet firm and authoritative.

"So, what do I do now?"

"What do you do? Absolutely nothing! Don't call her under any circumstances! If she wants to remain your fuck-buddy, the least she can do is make the move and come to you; that's the minimum, even though I'm not so sure that it's such a brilliant idea. The best thing by far is to forget all about her and move forward!"

Sure. I called her three days later.

"Hello."

"Merry?"

"I thought you'd call me." She made no effort to hide her satisfaction. "I'm sorry if I'm confusing you." Somehow this last statement didn't strike me as honest. I tried to think if I had mistreated her in a way that justified this abuse. I had met Merry through a friend. When I asked him if she was sexy, he answered that her body was soft and feminine. Soft and feminine it was. Merry is a sort of a Yemenite yuppie. The coffee has to be of a particular Italian brand and the wine served at such and such a temperature – her brothers claim that she is a wannabe Ashkenazi (In this context- An Israeli jew of European origin) betraying her Yemenite heritage. I fell in love with her when she first touched me. It was after our first date, a blind date. It was a nice date: where do you work, where were in the army, and so forth. Before we parted for the night, she put her hand on the muscle that connects my shoulder to my neck. She did this in order to lower me a little bit and kiss me on my cheek because she was roughly a head shorter than me, which means that she was pretty short. Electricity all over; some girls electrify you when they touch you. Romy's boyfriend told me that she had the same effect on him. He even gave specific details that were quite unnecessary – I'm not saying this out of jealousy. My friends keep nagging me about this: How is it possible that you don't try to make it with Romy? She loves you so much, this amazing girl, so what kind of a fool are you? they ask me. They don't understand that the idea of undressing her and squeezing her ample white breasts seems to me as reasonable as doing the same to my big sister. Still, even though we are platonic in the truest sense of the word, we do touch each other – bear hugs and empathetic pats. It's a great feeling to walk into a bar with her. The waitresses seem to treat me with immense respect because it's a well established fact that if you are with a very attractive woman, you must be extremely attractive yourself, no matter what you look like. In fact, I don't look that bad. I'm not great-looking; I'm cute, but a little too short. Could it be that Merry left me because of my friendship with Romy? I tried to clarify my relationship with Romy to her on numerous occasions and Romy also discussed this topic with her. We hardly touched each other in her presence in spite of the above-mentioned platonic nature of our intimacy. And yet, did I on occasion enjoy demonstrating our special kinship in her presence? Maybe I used Romy to hurt Merry when I was angry with her. Maybe she saw us bear-hugging when we didn't know she was around; them bear hugs can sometimes be quite misleading. Merry continued to show up at my door about once a week for the next three months. Then she started to date some other guy called Robby and I went into a fresh new crisis. It's a specialty of hers to leave me again and again and again.

The following week, I made it to the "Hey man, that's not bad!" level. Five months after that, five months of complete sexual drought it should be said in my defense, she reappeared in my apartment in the small hours. You must already rank me among the world's greatest suckers. Maybe. It could further be said in my defense that she caught me completely off guard. I was on my way to the springboard under the northeastern tower, where you find a cosmic shield that gives you total immunity from any weapons for twenty seconds. My nearly complete knowledge of the game is very pleasant – you could almost say that I have some intimacy with the game. I know where my four Roman emperors usually gather to fight among themselves. When I escape from one of them, I usually know where to go in order to draw them into a trap while being chased.

I know the damage caused by each weapon: I know for instance that the plasma and rockets are somewhat slow and enable you to escape even after they're launched straight at you, but they cause greater damage than the gun and machine-gun whose hit is instantaneous. I even know when the game is going to cheat me. Sometimes, when one of my dear emperors descends one of the staircases leading to the wall, I launch a salvo of rockets that is supposed to eradicate all memory of his existence right at him, and he leaps among them lightly as if it's gravel rather than heavy artillery I am throwing at him. Then I know that I'm going to be fucked no matter what I do or what he launches at me – destruction is certain.

Back to that tragic day on the northeastern tower. The problem with this tower is that it's taller than the other towers, and in order to reach the cosmic shield, you need two jumps rather than one. The first jump is executed with the springboard while the second is achieved with an energy pill that needs to be collected prior to the event. The platform on top is very small; there is hardly space to stand and you need to pick up the shield and get the hell out of there because the minute you get there, the whole empire opens fire in your direction. I was already on top of the tower, a split second away from obtaining the precious shield, when the doorbell rang. I froze because I was practically sure who was on the other side. My heart, which was blown into pieces as a result of having sustained a direct hit from three rockets, is yet to recover.

"How's Robby doing?"

"Who's Robby?"

"Are you sure this is a good idea?"

From this question, an intention to exercise discretion and get the hell rid of her might be implied. Alas, even as those words left my mouth, I was quite aware of the mental weakness backing them. Merry, too, recognized my feeble position and reached for the location where that weakness is concentrated. There is something terribly flattering about your ex coming for more again and again. Unfortunately, I am still in love with Merry and she knows that in some irrational corner of my mind, I still hope to bring her back to me, and that's why I don't date other women. Romy explained the secrets of female maneuvers to me in detail. She is amused by the games Merry is playing with me and tries to help me in the mental battle. Unfortunately, that does me no good. Does a fly benefit from understanding the structure of a spider web? Sometimes, after I am destroyed, one of my emperors – Julius, for instance – says:

"What a piece of shit!" and Claudius continues: "Not anymore!" and the "more" is said in a rising tone, relaying a stupid satisfaction. This definitely strengthens my suspicions that this whole game is nothing but a big conspiracy against me, since it is supposed to be a jungle where everybody fights everybody, which is what they do most of the time, but these combined insults do blacken the atmosphere and arouse my suspicions. Having been humiliated by Claudius, I resurrect. I have seven kills already, Claudius and Augustus have eight each, and Julius and Tiberius are way behind. I can smell the sweet smell of victory. I take a deep breath, maintain constant motion leftwards and rightwards, backwards and forwards, for in this game, he who stays put is kaput! I am in the inner court of the inner wall. I can hear the sounds of battle from afar and I know that I have to move to where the action is, otherwise in a minute or two I'll see the table telling me that I have finished in second place and a most obnoxious voice will thunder: "You lose, bitch!" I guess the programmers were real negative types. I don't understand why this game can't announce the news of my defeat in a more civilized manner. Isn't it enough of a humiliation to lose to this bunch of virtual morons?

I jump to the corner of the wall and pick up a machine-gun. Claudius is standing with his back to me, his attention directed at a fight with Julius. What a break! I aim, open fire right at the center of his back and what do you know?

"Die, motherfucker!" my computer shouts in my honor, and Claudius lies still in a puddle of his own blood. It's a pretty frustrating business that I can't curse them with my own mouth. The insults uttered by the computer on my behalf sound terribly similar to those directed against me, so there is no catharsis! I spot a rocket launched by Augustus in time and manage to jump off the wall and run around the corner as the rockets pass me by. The bell rings and I decide that today, nothing will take the sweet victory away from me! Alas, it's too late! In this one second of lack of concentration, Augustus sends a bluish plasma salvo right at me, the world spins around me, the computer announces with satisfaction: "What a useless piece of shit!", and the table telling me that Augustus is in first place and I am in second place appears. How could this possibly be? He only had eight kills before this one; where did he get another one? I

refuse to play this stupid game anymore! You probably realize that I have made this solemn commitment a thousand times, but I always return to the objects of my addiction. The bell rings again, but my sweet Merry doesn't utter a sound. Maybe I should wait for her to announce her presence verbally, that idiotic snob? I could wait a few more minutes and should she decide to go, that would be absolutely fantastic! But will she ever come back? Do I want her to come back? I certainly want to see her now; why should I deny myself what I desire? Am I a fool? Quite obviously. I open the door.

"Why are you so angry?" She is smiling, standing on five-inch heels, her soft and feminine body, the color of fresh coffee, wrapped in a long, tight, black dress. I would really like to tear that dress to pieces. I believe I have already explained that my attraction to her isn't based on looks alone. Merry is far from perfect; her legs are too short, which is why she feels obliged to wear such ridiculously high heels, and her ears are somewhat protruding, even though I have gotten used to that feature and have even developed a certain affection for her cute ears.

"You made me lose. I was on the verge of beating them at the 'Absolutely impossible' level."

"Are you mad at me or at the game? Actually the question is, which of us are you more mad at?" Merry smiles at me and pinches my cheek. I can feel warmth spreading across my cheek and sending octopus arms to various parts of my face. My eye twitches involuntarily. I bite my lower lip, trying instinctively to locate the source of this somewhat strange taste in my mouth.

"Why do you always show up in the middle of the night?" She spreads her hands sideways in a gesture of dismay as if she is the victim of *force majeure*. She passes by me on the way to the kitchen and rubs her thigh against mine – I am completely ready for action.

"Is there anything to eat in your fridge?" She takes a lemon-flavored yogurt.

"Make yourself at home," I say half-sarcastically – only half because if I had a personality, I would be a little firmer with her instead of being half-sarcastic.

"It's one of the nicest things about you, your constant readiness for unexpected visits."

"Believe it or not, the main reason for my keeping food in the fridge is so I can eat it."

"Umm."

"Shhh…." I try to talk, and utter a strange sound. I close my eyes and try to concentrate so I can find the right words. I suddenly remember that it's my parents' anniversary this week and I haven't bought anything yet. What shall I buy for my parents?

"We need to talk."

"Umm."

"It's been a year since we broke up now." I sit on my chair by the computer, but I sit kind of sideways, half turning toward Merry, who is busy consuming my yogurt by the kitchen door.

"Umm."

"What do you think about this year? All in all, looking back I think it was a pretty bad year."

"Ummm." Merry likes yogurt a lot.

"It's so very interesting to talk to you, ummm."

"I'm listening; so far I haven't had anything of any importance to say."

"Ummm."

"You've made tremendous progress with the game, haven't you? That's positive, isn't it?"

I am so stupid. Did I really think this conversation would get me anywhere? I should hang in there, politely show her the door, and go to sleep. And then what? Will that mean I'll never see her again? That I'm giving up the girl with whom I've had the best sex so far? The second place doesn't even come close. Merry taught me all about sex. Before meeting her, I would just squirm with frustration and She loves having sex with me; could there be a better combination? She is the coolest girl I've ever dated; she took me to my first trance party. Come to think of it, she's probably the first girl I've ever dated that's considered to be cool by the majority of the population.

That really boosted my self-confidence and it's probably the best demonstration of how unconfident I am. Some people would actually define her as sexy although opinions differ and there are several schools of thought regarding the definition of sexy. Does the relative shortness of my sweetheart's legs prevent her membership in the prestigious club?

We have had some good times, and I find myself engulfed in nostalgia. There was that week in the Greek islands.

We cruised peacefully from island to island, biking among archeological relics and picturesque villages. We reached a small village and we promised each other that we would come back for our honeymoon. This village was spread across two sides of a beautiful valley and a small stream flowed between them.

I can send Merry home and never see her again and end this weird existence I have been leading for the last year. That could be a good opportunity to quit this annoying game. It's amazing – whenever I play this game, I feel humiliated and yet I play it again and again. But if I quit now, I'll never win the tenth level. Winning the "I am in fucking awe man!" level is the supreme goal of the game. There is an Internet forum and if you win this level, you can send your victory file to the forum managers and in return, they send you a "Grand Fucking Master of the Universe" certificate or something of the sort. Obscenities are a crucial part of the forum ideology; it's a major part of the fresh, cool approach to life of us players.

So maybe I shouldn't say goodbye to Merry just yet. I can make a firm decision to break up with her should I fail to win her back as a girlfriend by the time I win the "I am in fucking awe man!" level. Perhaps the day after that, though – one should allow for a victory fuck. Having said that, isn't it a bit strange to think of breaking up with the woman who has already dumped me three times? I am in a dilemma, but I am too confused to define my dilemma.

Do I really believe in the chance to win her back or am I hooked on sex with her? Giving up the best sex ever isn't a light decision. Maybe I should leave things as they are for the meanwhile? It's not that bad, after all – there are a zillion people who are truly eager to have this kind of a deal. I get a world-class lay with no commitment and it's not just sex, there's intimacy involved as we have known each other for almost two years. I can rest my head on her breasts, close my eyes and lose myself under her soothing, caressing hands, and that's something you don't get from just any girl you meet in a bar. Not that it's so trivial to meet girls in a bar. I once got the phone number of a girl I met in a bar. A week later, we had a date and we slept together. It was quite horrible and that was the last I saw of her. There is a myth according to which any man can walk into a pickup bar in Tel Aviv and walk out with an eager lady by his side. That's not entirely accurate. I have a good friend who is a real stud. We tried to count all the girls he'd slept with and came out with a respectable one hundred and twelve! And of all the one hundred and twelve, only once in his life did he go home with a girl from a bar, and that was in Jerusalem!

All my friends tell me that they would love to have an arrangement like I have with Merry. Romy on the other hand tells me that in the last year, I have been wearing myself out and totally humiliating myself for some good sex and that I should leave the past behind and move forward. She is obviously right, but must it really happen now, this great move forward? Would it not be more fitting to carry out the move in my own good time? Today I almost won the "Absolutely impossible" level. Suppose I need another week to accomplish this task: so far I've won nine levels in twelve months, about forty days per level. Assuming that winning the "I am in fucking awe man!" level will be a little more difficult, I guess I can expect to finally defeat this game in about two months. Perfect! I will close two circles in my life and move forward from a position of victory and accomplishment rather than of defeat! My whole body relaxes as the full meaning of this courageous decision fills me with peace and tranquility. I have two more months to continue the fight against my dear emperors and enjoy the pleasures of the flesh. Mind you, I am far better off than those pathetic little kings. When I turn off the computer they sink into some sort of virtual hibernation and I am the only one who can then bring them back to life. I am the incarnation of omnipotence!

I am sitting with my back to Merry, kind of expecting her to surprise me with an unexpected touch or caress. I can hear her footsteps behind me, her hand slides near my cheek as she goes to put the empty yogurt cup on the table. I sniff her hand and two seconds later she grabs the muscle connecting my neck to my shoulder: I can feel this cozy tickle in my neck followed by an involuntary cramp in my stomach.

"Sweetie, I'm out of here, so have a good night."

"What?"

"I think we need some distance from each other. Maybe we should just stop meeting."

"Ahhhhh!" Why did I have to utter that ridiculous sound? It sounded like the cry of a pig that just heard he is about to be turned into spareribs. So humiliating! And the bitch is a mind-reader! I have to find a new game – in two weeks I'll finish off the Roman emperors, and then what will I do?

The Orange Mosquito Stories

1. The Orange Mosquito wants you to get married

I woke up in the middle of a winter night. Outside it was still pitch black and I tried to separate dream from reality and understand what had made me wake up at such an early hour. I looked at the other side of the bed and remembered that my girlfriend had gone to a hen party and wasn't supposed to return until dawn. I considered going back to sleep immediately before being completely seized by wakefulness, but I felt a slight itch in my right foot and I turned on the light. It only took a quick inspection to discover that I had been bitten by a mosquito. There is a strong temptation to fall asleep immediately in such a situation, hoping that the threat will just disappear, but I knew that this course of action might get me all bitten and itchy by morning. I stood up and began screening the walls, ceiling and other major expanses in the room. A nocturnal mosquito hunt can be either a fairly easy task or a long and frustrating experience. It's sheer luck that makes the difference. This time I was lucky. After a few seconds, I spotted the mosquito on the wall, about a meter to my right. I guess I was so exhausted that it took me some time to realize that this was no ordinary mosquito. An orange mosquito? Should I take its corpse to a hospital in the hope that they would be able to produce a serum and save me? Or perhaps capture it alive and take it to the zoo? Maybe they would name the new species after me. I moved a little bit closer to it and observed it.

It was a fairly large mosquito and had quite obviously dined recently. "We need to talk."

"We need to talk?"

I'm talking to an orange mosquito. When I was in Thailand I saw all kinds of mosquitoes. There was one that looked like a tiger with black and yellow stripes – really scary. One of these landed on my arm and if my girlfriend hadn't killed it in time, I might have caught Dengue fever. "We ought to discuss your condition."

Maybe I'm on something? Not very likely, I'm just not a chemical kind of guy. In Thailand, someone persuaded me to take a pill – I didn't even know what it was. It made me feel like an atom bomb and see all kinds of strange colors. That was a year ago. Maybe I'm experiencing a flashback. I once read that some types of drugs can repeat their strange phenomena a long time after usage – a sort of a chemical monster lurking in a dark corner of your brain waiting for the right moment to show up. I raised my gaze from one of the lovely flowers decorating my sheet back to the wall. I lashed out quickly in an attempt to surprise the mosquito, but I guess it was prepared for that one. It hovered for a few seconds and returned to a higher point on the wall.

"Don't do that! Don't you see that I am a special mosquito? Have a little respect! How many times have you encountered an orange mosquito?"

"You bit me, you blood-sucking parasite! What's so special about that?" I'm still talking to a mosquito.

"I'm sorry. Does it itch?"

"What do you think?" I shouted at it.

"I don't know, I've never been bitten by a mosquito."

"You're funny, aren't you?"

On that same trip to Thailand, I had a totally unpleasant encounter with other members of its species.

My girlfriend and I were on our way to our guesthouse. We were in the middle of a fight; I'm not sure what it was about. Maybe she caught me staring at a particularly attractive Swedish tourist. Maybe the Swedish tourist was another time. We were walking irritably on the beach. I don't deal with pressure very well so this was a very stressful walk for me. Whenever I fight with my girlfriend, it feels like the world is coming to an end. Occasionally I tried to say something, but she gave me the silent treatment. My concentration on her and her silence was so complete that I didn't pay any attention to what was going on with my body. Suddenly, a few minutes before we reached the guesthouse, I felt a terrible itch. It was a sharp transition from total numbness to an accentuated awareness of every square centimeter of my body, as if my physical awareness mechanism had been switched on after a short break. On my neck, behind my ears, on my hands and feet – anything that was exposed itched terribly. I began scratching myself like a madman, troubled with thoughts of tropical diseases. It took me a while to realize what was going on with me – I had been bitten from head to toe. I looked around me and didn't see any mosquitoes. Then I thought I heard a buzz over my head. I looked up and was amazed by what I saw: hovering above me was a two-meter-wide cloud of mosquitoes. I have never seen anything quite like it. It resembled the swarms of allied bombers over the German cities. I began running like a maniac, waving my hands and clapping them over my head. I looked at my hands and they were smeared with bleeding mosquito corpses.

We ran to our room and my girlfriend rubbed my body with lots of tiger balm lotion. You might say that the mosquito attack brought reconciliation. She obviously couldn't go on being mad at me in my badly bitten condition. I was grateful for her treatment and besides, I hadn't wanted this fight in the first place.

"You see?"

"I see what?"

"In Thailand, who brought you guys together again? I lost some good friends in that peaceful mission."

I suddenly realized that this mosquito wasn't talking to me. It was transmitting its thoughts to me and reading my thoughts. So how come I had almost managed to kill it? It should have identified my hostile intentions in advance and escaped before I administered the blow.

"It was spontaneous. Even you were surprised by that shameless effort."

"What is it you want from me?"

"I want you to get married."

The orange mosquito wants me to get married? That is one strange mosquito.

"Tell me the truth. That fight you had on the way to your guesthouse – do you honestly believe it was about a little peek at some tourist?"

"I'm not sure. Maybe the Swedish tourist was another time. Perhaps this fight was over food. I persuaded her to go to a seafood restaurant I looked up in the guide. She wanted to go have a pizza or a hamburger. I worked pretty hard to convince her that we hadn't traveled all the way to Thailand to eat junk food. We were sitting in the backyard of the restaurant, eating a spicy shrimp soup called Tom Yum Kung followed by a delicious fish topped with a crispy layer of garlic. Everything was great, but my girlfriend got terrible heartburn – the Thai cook put lots of chili in the soup – and she gave me an angry look for every moan of delight I uttered. Besides, there were many mosquitoes in that illuminated yard, but they were pretty easy to spot and the damage was limited. Come to think of it, I don't think they touched her, only me."

"Sure, we were trying to move your sorry ass from that restaurant to a Pizza Hut.

Why should your girlfriend suffer the results of your selfishness? But that's not the point. Do you honestly believe you guys were fighting over food? Think again!"

"Look, I know that there are far more basic problems in our relationship, but that doesn't mean we can't fight over nonsense like any normal couple."

"Oh, cut the crap, will you? How long have you been together now, huh?"

"Five years."

"And how old is your girlfriend?"

"She's 30."

"And what do you think she wants?"

"She wants to get married. So what? I don't feel ready for that kind of commitment. Besides, we've been living under the same roof for three years now – we're just like a married couple."

Explaining myself to a mosquito was definitely a very low point in my life.

"Not quite. The way things are now, you can leave her in five seconds."

"Getting married won't change that. Married couples break up all the time."

"When you have kids it becomes more difficult."

"Now you want me to have kids? Don't you think you're just a little bit out of line here? I mean, for Christ's sake, I don't even know you."

"You need to stop this irresponsible existence of yours. You're thirty-five now. How many more years are you going to shut your eyes and live like there's no tomorrow, huh? Get a grip on yourself!"

A split second before my hand squished the poor bastard, I managed to pick up its last thought:

"You'll regret this!"

I looked at the wall expecting to find orange mosquito remains – something that resembled a slaughtered carrot.

I saw a red spot, the same as with every other slain mosquito. Had there been an orange mosquito in the first place? I decided to forget the whole thing and share this with no one. Still, it had a point, didn't it? Ah, such nonsense!

The alarm clock rang at exactly seven a.m. I stretched my arms, buried my head in the pillow and carefully reached out for the right side of the bed. She wasn't there – probably continued directly to breakfast with the other party girls. Suddenly I got a little worried. Maybe I should call her? It's not like her to disappear on me like this, without even leaving a message.

I got up, took a quick shower and washed some fruit for breakfast. I always start the day with some fruit and tea and cake for dessert. Only when I was drinking my tea did I remember the orange mosquito and try to decide whether it had appeared in a dream or in reality. I went to my room and looked at the wall. The red spot was still there. I usually clean the wall after hunting a mosquito (if you don't clean it right away, it's hard to get rid of the stain), but this time I was too tired. Strange, I guess at least some of it really happened. Why was my girlfriend so late? I called her and after a few rings, I heard her sweet voice telling me to leave a message after the beep. Where was she? Maybe it really was time we got married. It should be noted that I have never been bitten by a mosquito since.

2. The stripper

Standing in front Ms Manor's door, I didn't imagine that this time would be any different from other. I have probably done this a thousand times already. I come to the apartment, do my thing and stay a little bit longer if it's really nice. Sometimes I don't leave alone. Occasionally someone slips me her phone number or ambushes me on my way out. If I really like her, we might go home and have a ball, but in most cases, I politely decline – very politely, because the reputation of a creep will ruin me in my present line of work.

Three years ago, I was a computer programmer. I worked fourteen hours a day and daydreamed of wealth and fortune. A few months after the hi-tech crisis, our company went bankrupt, my imagined wealth vanished, and I suddenly found myself unemployed and facing terrible competition for every job offer. My stripping days began after a talk with my good friend Sean. Actually, he suggested I work as a gigolo, not seriously, of course – "With your looks, you could probably earn ten times your salary as a programmer." After some thought, I concluded that he had a point. But having sex for money, that's a little too corrupt for me. It wasn't easy to make the decision. Sometimes on my way to a girl's party, in the few meters I have to walk from the cab to the house, I run into people. When they see my big arms and broad shoulders, my exquisite features and provocative outfit – bear in mind that this happens late at night – they usually guess my line of work more or less. Where men are concerned, the reaction is the same almost every time. Their bodies stiffen and they assume a defensive position against a clear and present danger to their existence.

At such times, I almost feel that I can read their minds – they are totally convinced that I fulfill their wildest fantasies since I exist in another world, the world of eternal lust and pleasure and they would never guess that I am an ordinary man just like they are and that in many cases I'd rather stay at home with a good book than dance naked in front of a bunch of strange girls. It's not so simple to enter an apartment crammed with suspicious women and breathe normally and function. Most men think that I have to radiate uninhibited sexuality, try to seduce them and drive them crazy. Sex has obviously got a lot to do with it, but the first thing I try to do upon arrival is make everybody feel comfortable and let them know that friendly forces have just entered the premises, otherwise the whole night can turn ugly. Words of praise for the interior design are a proven icebreaker. However, I only use this technique when my admiration is real; phony compliments rarely work.

This time, my compliments were justified. The living room was beautiful, all furnished with second-hand junk, but those are my favorite living rooms. I am sometimes invited to houses in Savion or other such places where you always find zillion-dollar living rooms – Italian leather couches worth a whole year's salary, gigantic mirrors that cover entire walls. I always compliment the owners, but I know that it's the designer who deserves the credit. I think I can already identify the designer in most cases. Anyway, having seen this living room, I was sure that I would get along wonderfully with the bride-to-be, who happened to own the place. By the television there was a bookcase, and among the books there was a little fat black Buddha and other Oriental stuff. Above the bookcase was a shelf on which stood two rather big colorful wooden parrots staring at each other, and a ceramic cat.

I looked at the old couches that were tastefully cushioned and at the round black coffee table standing on a reddish carpet, both of which had been moved to make room for the partying girls.

I tried to understand what it was that made this living room, which did not contain a single article of exceptional quality, into such an aesthetic and pleasant space. The drapes were pretty simple, but they looked wonderful above the couches, and the long Chinese scroll by the window also contributed to the harmony. I noticed that almost everything was asymmetrical. On the other side of the window there was a blue vase with some dried flowers standing on a little shelf, and the little ornaments among the books were also in apparent disorder and yet matched their surroundings perfectly.   It's all completely beyond me. I am deeply interested in the aesthetics of a collection of objects in a given space. It has always fascinated me. What is it about my face that causes so many people, men included, to find it beautiful, to stop in the middle of the street and stare? I have to admit that in spite of my conviction that I possess deeper qualities than beauty, I sometimes find myself standing in front of the mirror for minutes at a time, admiring myself, thinking how lucky I am and how delightful it is to know that I look like this. Quite clearly, unlike the living room, the secret of my looks has got nothing to do with asymmetry. But what is it? What is it about this arrangement of a nose, eyes, a mouth, ears, a forehead, cheekbones and hair, organs possessed by the majority of men, that makes me more handsome than others?

My friend Sean, who launched me into this weird career, is terribly jealous of me even though he is quite good-looking. He usually hangs out with pretty women. I can get prettier girls, so what? Sean dumps his girlfriends after six months on average. His relationships work more or less in a fixed pattern. In the first few weeks, he is hopelessly in love. A few months later, we might be sitting in a bar or walking along the promenade by the sea, and he starts complaining about some part of her that's not perfect: maybe her breasts are too small or her face a little too crude or her skin not dark enough or not white enough – it doesn't really matter. He has this inner clock that's wound up whenever he likes someone. It takes approximately six months for him to transfer his self-hatred to his unfortunate partner. Sounds shallow? Maybe. But that's my conclusion following years of observation. Unsatisfactory looks are his most common excuse, but not the only one. Lack of finesse is another option. I have seriously considered making a move with more than one of his ex-girlfriends who have just been dumped, but I have never actually done it because I am afraid it would end our friendship. I know that five seconds after I start dating his ex, she will become the epitome of perfection and I will be the evil man who stole his happiness. Sometimes I wonder if I am the source of his misery; would he be a happier man if he hadn't met me?

Having surveyed and admired the living room, I looked around trying to locate the bride-to-be, who had let me in and then disappeared on me. I watched the girls, most of whom were dancing. Occasionally one of them glanced at me or gave me a smile, but none of them engaged. I went into the kitchen and there she was, standing by the sink, adding some pecans to the salad.

"There you are. Shall I start now or a little bit later?"

"Could you wait a little while? It's just that... well, you said you'd give one hour. Is it OK if you begin a little later? You can eat in the meantime, there's lots of food."

"Sure, I'm in no hurry, I can even give a longer show if that makes everybody happy."

"Really? For no extra charge?"

"Sure, not a shekel more."

It embarrasses me tremendously when my female clients think of me in the same terms they think of a prostitute.

"I must tell you that this apartment is great." I went on to explain very sincerely what it was that made me like her living room so much.

"Is that so? In that case I should introduce you to Maya. Who knows, maybe you'll be the fortunate man to end her misery."

I wondered what this Maya girl would think of that and it kind of put me on edge. She disappeared for a few seconds and came back with Maya. I smiled and thought that I'd actually be delighted to put an end to whatever it was that was making her miserable. I have seen prettier women in my life and I have slept with sexier girls, but she had clever deep bluish eyes and wonderfully broad hips that were wrapped in some sort of flowered sarong. Like the living room she had designed, there was a harmony in her clothes that I couldn't quite define, but it was definitely there.

"Meet Ram, the main attraction."

"Really?" Maya seemed truly amazed.

"Yup, that's me." I smiled and offered my hand.

"By the way, Maya is the celebrated designer of my humble home, so she deserves all the positive thoughts you had for me."

We exchanged pleasantries and compliments and when the bride-to-be was at a safe distance, I said:

"I'm not sure that I should repeat this to you, but Mademoiselle Manor asked me to relieve your misery and you don't seem like a miserable person, not even a little bit." There is no doubt that I abused Ms Manor's trust, but apparently even I tend to lose my cool around particularly desirable women.

"Ummm, remind me to kill her at the end of the evening."

"Oh no, please don't kill her. Kill me or else tell her how I betrayed her trust and then she'll kill me."

"OK. You're nice, Ram. I didn't think we'd have such a nice stripper. Are you really going to dance naked for us?"

"Yup, but don't worry, everybody is going to have fun."

"That's great then."

"And you should know that I won't be completely naked."

I started mingling with the girls. There was a seventeen-year-old girl with a purple bob and a little pigtail. She was the sister of one of the bride's friends and I was quick to make friends with her because everybody knows that the young ones in the crowd are the real key to people's hearts. Actually, it was quite easy. She was at the stage in a girl's life where she feels nothing but contempt for the rest of the world, but quite obviously, a cool and pretty thing such as myself dissolved that contempt in a flash, and after about two seconds, we were best friends. I spent a few more minutes joking with some of the girls – just enough to direct that critical mass of good will toward me – and then I took my bag, went into the bathroom, and changed into my working outfit. I peeked out of the bathroom and the bride was waiting just outside.

"Are you ready? Should I start the music?"

"Yup, go ahead."

"There's no stage or table you can use, but I moved all the girls to one side of the room, so you'll have enough space to dance and… do whatever it is you do."

"To which side did you move them – the side nearer to or further from the bathroom?"

"Nearer. You'll have to pass through them to reach your side. Is that a problem?"

"No problem whatsoever."

"OK then, good luck."

"Thanks, and don't worry, everything's gonna be just fine."

I winked at her and kissed her on the cheek and she smiled and I wondered when I had acquired this ability to look so confident when I was anything but. OK, here we go. I walked out of the bathroom, covered the three meters to the living room, and entered with totally exaggerated moves – I always use this trick to ease everybody's tension a little bit, especially my own. I stood with my hand stretched up like young John Travolta and everybody cheered and yelled. I began making my way through the girls to my side of the room. The girls made way for me and I began shaking my body with a lot more style. With Eminem cursing his mother in the background, I took off the necktie that's always the first item to come off and gave it to the purple girl while gently putting my arm around her and kissing her sweet cheek. Everybody began to scream and some girls shouted, "Hey, careful with our baby!" and similar remarks. By the time I reached the other side of the room, I had already been lightly caressed by some girls, most of whom were quite attractive, and I responded to a couple of them with light caresses and kisses. I'm always very careful, because if you touch a girl in a way that offends her, a happy night can turn into a disaster with criminal implications. I tried to spot Maya, with no luck. I reached my territory and began my routine: a sort of sexy dance that involves discarding items of clothing every once in a while. When I was left wearing a tiny pair of pants, everybody made the bride dance with me, as they usually do. There have been times when the bride-to-be was so drunk and crazy that I had to cool her off – I have my ethics and fucking the bride-to-be is totally out of the question. This time I knew there would be no such problem – I could feel that I had been brought to please her guests and she wasn't really into it. I did a relaxed dance with her and afterwards I exposed my elephant underwear.

The trunk covers my dick and the head covers my balls and its unveiling is an event that always draws wild cheers from the crowd. After a wild Lambada with one of the girls, I finished the show, mainly because I could see they were beginning to lose interest. All in all, it had been quite a pleasant evening so far. I collected my clothes, which were scattered all over the place, hugged and kissed some of the girls, and went to the bathroom to get dressed and be alone for a minute or two. When I came out of the bathroom, I saw Maya, who was just coming out of the toilet.

"Hey, how are you?"

"I'm fine." She had a beautiful smile.

"Are you OK?"

"I'm just great. I hope you didn't suffer. Somehow I got the feeling you'd rather listen to a string quartet than see my uncivilized show. I hardly saw you." I think I said that with the disappointed tone of a five-year-old who didn't get his ice cream. She laughed and said:

"I'm sorry, I just wasn't in the right mood." She moved closer to me and I was almost sure that she was going to kiss my neck. The fine scent of her hair filled my nostrils.

"Your neck is quite red."

"Red?"

"While you were dancing, the mosquitoes were killing you." Two seconds after she said that, I began to feel itchy all over: on my neck, on my back, behind my elbows, on my knees – it was terrible. I took a deep breath and drew her wonderful smell into my stomach.

"You're right. I was so focused on my show that I didn't feel anything. I'd better go home and have a shower."

"A shower won't do you any good. Come to the balcony." I did as I was ordered. We sat down and she pulled out a little hexagonal bottle with a yellow lotion inside.

"What's that?" "That's Tiger Balm lotion," she said without any further explanations. Then she took a long pointed nail and stuck it into the juiciest mosquito bite at the back of my arm, right above my elbow. "Ouch!"

"Shhh." She opened the bottle, heaped a little pile of lotion on her nail and rubbed it on the bite. At first I felt nothing. She repeated the same routine bite after bite and I began to feel a pleasant sensation of heat that spread from the infected areas and made me stop feeling the itch. It's such a great feeling to be taken care of and I watched her expression of concentration as she rubbed lotion and searched my skin for potential disaster areas. She had the Scandinavian look – her hair was pale blonde, almost white, and it cascaded down her back through a red kerchief that might have looked old on someone else, but looked just right on her.

"You're staring at me."

"Yeah, I guess you're right. I'm sorry."

"It's OK, I forgive you. Does your back itch? Do you want to take off your shirt?"

"You'd do that for me? That's so nice of you. My back itches terribly and I was afraid to ask." I took off my shirt and she resumed the rescue operations.

"Your back is bitten beyond recognition. I have never seen a back so badly bitten."

"I gather you have lots of experience with bitten backs."

"My boyfriend also has this tendency to get bitten, especially when we're traveling in exotic places."

Ah, her boyfriend, I thought painfully, and it suddenly became very clear to me that I wanted Maya in a most desperate way, not just sexually, I wanted us to take care of each other day and night until our last day on this planet, or maybe, I thought, I was just a prick who wanted a woman the minute he learned that she belonged to someone else. I sighed, closed my eyes and completely succumbed to the gentle fingers rubbing and stinging me and the wonderful warm sensation in the rubbed spots.

"You've got plenty of back, definitely a mosquito's paradise." She gave my shoulder a light caress as she said that and I felt the heat there as well. "Now let's do your stomach."

"I've got to tell you – and I do hope you'll forgive me – your boyfriend is a very lucky man. Really, I'm extremely jealous of him."

"Ahhhh." She sighed as she was rubbing the last bites.

"What's wrong?"

"Well, it's just that… maybe you should explain to him how lucky he is. We've been together for five years and he still doesn't know what he wants."

"Such an idiot! I mean, I'm sorry, who am I…"

"It's OK, you're absolutely right, though maybe it's me who's the idiot."

"Say, I hope I don't stink after all that dancing. I sweat like a pig."

"No, actually your smell is great, marvelous," she said, and clapped her hands just above my head.

"Ah, we've got the villain. Look at all that blood – I think I've got your entire blood supply on my hand." As she said this, her face was about an inch from mine and suddenly she kissed me lightly on my mouth and smiled.

"Tell me, do you want to go somewhere when this party is over, which is more or less now?"

"Are you sure? I really do want to go with you, I want to desperately, but I don't want you to remember me as the bastard stripper who tried to ruin your life. If we do go somewhere, just promise me one thing, OK? Promise me that we won't have sex tonight because I like you so much and I don't want this to turn into another one-night stand."

"I'm not promising you anything." She kissed me again.

This time the kiss was a little bit longer and the tip of her tongue touched the tip of mine.

"But I promise you that if we screw today, it doesn't mean that this has to be a one-night stand. I mean, we are in the twenty-first century, huh?"

And that's how I met my wife. When asked how we met, I tell people that we were brought together by a mosquit

3. Oh brother, my chakra is blocked

"Can you see it now?"

"Yup."

"Where is it? I definitely can't see it."

"I know you can't see it. I may be delusional, but I'm not completely crazy. Besides, it's sitting on your face, above your right eyebrow." Doctor Matthews shifted awkwardly in his chair and wiped his forehead with his hand.

"It's OK, there's nothing on your face. I hope I'm not contagious."

"Right. Since when have you had this problem?"

It all began on a flight back to Israel from Amsterdam. (To be quite honest, it probably started a few days earlier.) I was sitting in my tiny space trying to squeeze my long legs into the ridiculous gap between my seat and the seat of the poor bastard sitting in the next row. Lunch was set out before me, waiting to be eaten: slices of chicken in mustard sauce with some rice, carrots and peas. And a spider! A spider? I screamed and hit the lunch tray, and it flew away and landed in the aisle. The woman sitting next to me, fortysomething and ultra-Orthodox, stared suspiciously at me.

"I had a huge spider in my tray; didn't you see it?"

She didn't bother to answer me. Meanwhile, the flight attendant showed up:

Are you OK sir?

No, I'm not, I said angrily.

I had a huge spider in my lunch tray.

A spider? The flight attendant gave me a strange look.

Yeah, a spider. I'm sorry about the mess.

Here, I'll help you clean up. Oh no, sir, it's OK.

Her tone softened a bit and I felt like a legitimate member of the human race again. Other passengers began looking around nervously in search of my monster. The flight attendant finished cleaning up my chicken and veggies, announced that no spider had been detected, and went to fetch me another lunch tray. I lifted the aluminum cover and barely managed to avoid repeating my previous performance because there it was again, among the slices of chicken and carrot. A blue spider? I took a deep breath, closed my eyes, and rubbed my eyelids with the back of my hands. When I opened my eyes again, was it gone? Not quite. It took a few seconds for it to materialize. I'm having hallucinations, I figured. In Amsterdam, I had consumed some bizarre chemicals, not just grass. I had also eaten some strange mushrooms I bought in a smart shop. My excuse for this irresponsible introduction of unknown materials into my body was that you only live once, etc., and there was Bar, of course. And now I was seeing a big blue spider – as big as an average tarantula – on my chicken. I looked at it and realized that it didn't exactly look like a spider. It wasn't just the blue color, even though it did have the basic attributes of a spider – eight legs, etc. It's just that it had a different quality to it. It's like the computer-animated characters in Walt Disney movies that look different from old-fashioned cartoons and from the real thing – they look more plastic and perfect than real things. This spider looked like none of the above – it looked almost transparent, although I couldn't see through it and the blue color was a lot more uniform than the color of a real live thing.

I peeked at the religious woman, who was sitting completely still. Her neck was frozen in an unnatural position and she was staring intently straight ahead. I guess I had scared her terribly, poor thing. I looked at my tray, picked up the knife and fork and wondered what was going to happen now. I lowered my knife toward the spider, moved the knife right through it and... it moved or rather vanished for a split second – I didn't exactly notice when – and rematerialized in my glass. I closed my eyes and suddenly felt a splitting headache; I was having a panic attack.

I am thirty years old; my life so far has been generally satisfactory. I have always been proud of my ability to know my limits: drink enough to enjoy myself, but not too much, smoke some grass without becoming constantly high, etc., drive carefully – it always amazes me how irresponsibly people drive, as if their lives were completely worthless. And there, in Amsterdam, for the sole purpose of impressing the rather young guys I was hanging out with, especially the 21-year-old Bar with whom I was having an affair, I forgot all the rules and abandoned my principles for a sweet girl. Didn't I tell everybody that I wasn't going to touch unknown chemicals? Such a spineless idiot! And maybe it's not the mushroom; maybe I have a brain tumor or something. I remembered a scene from *Allie McBeale*, when a lawyer starts seeing imaginary dwarfs and a tumor is diagnosed. I emitted a little cough followed by another little cough and suddenly I was choking as if something was stuck in my throat, even though I hadn't eaten anything.

"Sir, are you OK?"

The sympathetic flight attendant was standing next to me. I tried to take a deep breath and told her breathlessly that I was fine. I cautiously looked at my tray again and what do you know? The spider was gone! I was overwhelmed with joy and enjoyed my meal as if I were eating in a three-star French restaurant.

So was it all a weird dream? The unfortunate answer came when I went to the bathroom. I usually like being a big tall guy, but it becomes a problem in the claustrophobic seats of those charter flights and in those tiny toilet cabins; it's a real nightmare. Jetliner toilets always make me feel tense and that makes me spend more time in them.

This, in turn, draws loud protests from other passengers waiting in line, which obviously gets me even more tense. I always feel that the small space is too limited for my big body and that the plastic walls around me are too thin to separate me from the angry crowd on the other side. Of course, I don't ever expose this weakness to any of the assholes waiting on line, but sometimes I have to wipe my sweaty forehead in order to keep up appearances. After a few moments of waiting that seemed like hours – there is nothing like waiting in line for a jetliner toilet to stretch time like chewing gum – I entered the toilet cabin, closed the door behind me, and went ahead with the important task of lining the toilet seat in the hope of not catching a contagious disease. I sat down and moved my long legs awkwardly about the little place. My nervousness made me forget that other incident, so you might imagine how surprised I was to find the blue spider waiting on the toilet door. I screamed, the plane began to shake and I thought that if this turned out to be major air turbulence, I might end my life hacked into little pieces and covered with shit and blue spider remains. Yup, you can definitely say that I don't like to fly, and since 9/11, I've also been afraid that an angry Arab will hurl me into a fucking windmill in Amsterdam or into the Azrieli Towers on the way back to Israel. For a second I thought I heard it say:

"Hey, what's the problem? I'm your blue spider, don't you recognize me?" And I wondered whether my spider could talk as well, which was quite ridiculous, given the fact that it was a figment of my imagination in the first place. Even so, I concluded that talking was not an integral part of this hallucination and that the words I was supposedly hearing originated in another compartment of my brain and not from the part that had produced this multi-legged delusion.

The spider stood still and I decided to ignore it and continue with my business.

Alas, I was too nervous to function, and after a while, I looked at my watch and saw that I had already been in the toilet for ten minutes. I was afraid that the passengers and crew were all waiting beyond the door, and I began to sweat. Relax, I told myself, you were a tank commander in the army and now you're going to overcome this psychosomatic constipation. That didn't help, but luckily, at some point in time, I began to fantasize about Bar and what we had done together and temporarily forgot my hardship. Suddenly, I began to feel my extra load leaving me. Before leaving the toilet, I had to wash my face quite extensively because I was totally covered with sweat, but I managed to face the crowd in a fairly calm frame of mind. As I stepped out of the little cabin, I peeked inside again to see if the spider was still there, and there it was, blue as ever on the door. This made me wonder whether it would have been there if I hadn't looked inside, which was obviously impossible, because how could my hallucination exist in a flying toilet if I wasn't there to produce it? Maybe my spider had become independent.

"Don't tell me you're going in there again!" said a nasty little prick, and his equally ugly brother began to laugh. I mustered all the toughness I had inside me and gave him a mean look. He looked at me from down there and shut his mouth! I usually don't use my size against other people – in fact, I avoid it on principle – but every once in a while, if they are extraordinarily rude to me, it's nice to be able to frighten them with an angry look.

"May I make a suggestion?"

"Sure, that's why I'm here, to hear your ideas."

"What do you know about meditation?"

"Is that your suggestion, that I meditate?" I gave him a suspicious look.

"I don't know how."

"Well, I know a nice lady who gives meditation courses and I know that she intends to start a new group. I don't know if that will help you, but she's a smart woman with lots of feminine intuition, and she has helped many people already."

"Aren't you supposed to help me? What can she do that you can't?"

"This course is a very special experience; it's not like talking to a therapist. I just don't think I can solve your problem. I will send you to do a scan just to be on the safe side, but I don't really believe that you have a brain tumor or anything like that. This course costs about the same as two appointments with me and I don't think that meeting me will help you at this stage. You go there and we'll be in touch and... who knows, maybe she can help you with your flying toilet problem."

"You really think so?"

"Maybe. When you meditate, you learn to find a certain peace of mind, learn how to keep the world out of your system. She talks about all kinds of spiritual stuff – you don't have to buy all that, you can just take what's good for you."

A few days later, I was in the living room of Emilia, the meditation instructor. Emilia spoke excellent Hebrew with a strong Argentinean accent. She was about 50. Her living room was quite spacious and most of the furniture had been moved to make room for the mattresses that were spread all over the floor. Besides Emilia and me there were two boys and two girls. Mily was a big girl – tall, wide and rather robust – and Anna was really small, maybe five foot tall, and terribly cute. She had curly golden hair and the deep blue color of her eyes was much nicer than the blue of my spider. The two men seemed to be on the verge of a mental breakdown. I guess people with real problems come to this place.

Emilia told us to stand up, and we did some warm-up and breathing exercises. Then we sat down.

Each one introduced himself and his problem, and when it was my turn, I realized with dismay that concentrating on other people's stories had made me forget my spider. Before I started talking, I did what had become a new bad habit: when I didn't see my spider, I looked for it. I'm not sure why; maybe knowing where it was made me feel I had some control over my new madness. This time I found it standing on a big blue clock hanging on the wall, and it kind of blended in with the background.

My name is Adam, I introduced myself, and my problem is… I hesitated, not knowing what kind of response I would get. Oh well, what the heck, I see a blue spider. You what? Emilia gave me an inquisitive but friendly look and everybody began to laugh, except for Tal, who had recently been dumped by his girlfriend. He asked me with a truly amazed expression on his face:

Are you sure it wasn't orange?

This world is just too strange sometimes! The other man, Danny, who had also been dumped recently, had developed a serious addiction to computer games.

Would you like to explain what you mean?

Emilia asked, and I described my problem and its history. And do you see it now, Mily asked curiously. Sure, I said, are you all nuts?

Don't you see that there's a blue spider on the big clock?

Everybody laughed and I got the feeling that they didn't take me very seriously.

I know this sounds funny, I said, but actually it's quite disturbing and I would really like to get rid of this virtual insect. After the introduction phase, we moved on to an hour of theory.

Emilia gave us some printed sheets and explained the Indian theory according to which there are seven chakras in our body. Spiritual energy flows through those chakras and if the flow is smooth, we're doing OK, but if the chakras are blocked, we're in trouble. All this spirituality was a bit too much for me and I remembered the psychiatrist's words about taking only what was good for me.

Anyway, I decided it would be appropriate to disclose my skepticism, so I told everybody that I didn't believe in chakras and spiritual energy. Emilia didn't take it too hard, but all the others gave me suspicious looks, as if I just told them that I believed the earth to be a big plate lying on a turtle's back rather than a sphere. Anna gave me a curious smile and I thought she was quite sexy in spite of her being so small and that it would be nice if I managed to get involved with her. The other three seemed terribly antagonized by my last remark and Emilia was quick to comment that there was nothing wrong with that; we were all entitled to have our own beliefs, and who knows, maybe by the end of the course I would change my mind. Who knows? I know! But I decided that from now on, I would not make an issue out of my skepticism.

Having finished the theoretical phase, we began our first meditation. We all lay down on the mattresses and closed our eyes. Whale music was playing in the background, and Emilia told us a story about our chakras, through which energy flows like the water of Lake Tiberias flows through the pipes of the National Water Carrier. Emilia explained beforehand that we were supposed to empty our heads of any thoughts, and I found it to be quite a paradox, wasting all that energy on thinking about how to stop thinking. Our empty mind is supposed to be bathed by a stream of visions and spiritual energy from our subconscious, and that should help us get in touch with ourselves or something of that nature. In spite of the difficulty, I managed to relax at some point, and when we finished meditating (if that's indeed what I did – I couldn't really say), I felt as though I had come out of a trance, but I was quite relaxed and I felt as if the exhaustion accumulated during the entire day was gone. After we all stretched and regained full consciousness, Emilia asked who would like to describe his experience and how it related to the reason he had come to the course in the first place.

"Adam, would you like to start?"

"No, it's just that I'm not sure what to say" – because the stupid things I had seen weren't even remotely connected to anything.

"What did you go through? Did you get into it or were you too preoccupied with your spider? I'm not accusing you of anything, OK? Would you like to talk later?"

"No, it's OK. I'm not even sure I meditated. The first thing I saw was dripping water; I guess it's the ocean music that made me see that. Then I saw a big bowl of apples…"

I told them all the ridiculous things I had seen, which included all kinds of food. I guess I was rather hungry and toward the end I had seen a complete buffet. That made everybody laugh, including sweet Anna, who asked me whether I had seen salmon and cream cheese sandwiches or puff pastry with goose liver paté. No such luck, but she seemed very friendly indeed and that made me very happy. However, I was quite sure that none of this would help me with the spider, and I concluded that this place offered nothing more than a good time. Then Emilia surprised me: "I see you didn't really deal with your problem, but I did think about this fascinating enigma and I would like to share my thoughts with you. Shall we do it now or do you want to talk later in private?" Emilia was sitting crossed-legged and her warm brown eyes looked at me out of an ageless face that was covered with leathery skin. Her big breasts were directed right at me. I suddenly felt my crotch getting warmer –a woman with presence.

"It's OK. Go right ahead." I think the way I said it might have betrayed my low expectations.

"OK, let's start with the plane. Why did your spider make its first appearance on the plane? You took the suspicious mushroom a few days before, right?"

But of course!

Why did I need this spiritual lady to make me understand something so obvious?

"You said that your spider is blue, right?" lovely Anna asked.

"Yup."

"Maybe you saw it on the plane because it serves in the airforce." Everybody laughed. "Maybe, but I actually think that the reason why I first saw it on a plane was because I have a fear of flying."

"And yet you fly?"

"No choice, I'm afraid. I like to travel."

"Why are you afraid to fly?"

"Why?" I could never understand people who aren't afraid of flying. "Have you ever given any thought to what a miserable piece of tin a plane is? You have so many complicated systems that need to function simultaneously for the plane to keep flying, so many microchips, so many signals that might cause you to crash if they go wrong, so many people whose mistakes could kill you, and we just sit there like idiots, eating lunch or watching a movie like nothing could happen to us."

"OK, I think we understand why of all places to start seeing the spider, it was on the plane," Emilia said smiling, and everybody laughed. I think I had gotten into the role of the course clown – whatever I said or was said about me seemed to evoke laughter.

"And when you spoke about all those delicacies you saw when you meditated, well, maybe it's no surprise that it first appeared when you were eating. You're a hungry individual, aren't you? Were you very hungry then?"

"I guess so, but the spider really made me lose my appetite."

Everybody giggled. What had I said?

"But I'm really not sure that has anything to do with it."

"According to this theory, I should have seen it in the toilet first, because that's the most stressful location on the plane for me.

"Anyway, even if you're right, how does that help me?"

"Be patient, my friend. Maybe we can understand this spider bit by bit until we understand it completely."

"And then will it go away?"

"I hope so, but I can't promise you that." Emilia must have noticed my eyes searching for the spider.

"Is he still with us?"

"Yeah," I told her, "it's on you."

"Really? Where?"

"You don't want to know," and everybody laughed. Actually it was sitting on her nose with one leg stuck in her left nostril. Afterwards we walked to our cars together, Anna and I.

"I'm so envious of you. Do you really see a blue spider?"

"Yeah. Is that a reason to envy me?"

"Yeah, it's amazing. Seeing something that's not really there. It's like... well, it's like seeing aliens or something; there aren't many people who get to see stuff like that."

"Do me a favor, huh? The spider is quite enough. If I start seeing aliens, that'll really be the end for me." She laughed. "Sorry." Anna wore shoes with huge platforms, but she was still some twelve inches shorter than me, and I suggested that we sit on a bench.

"It's OK, it must be great being so tall. Me, even with these skyscraper shoes, I still have to look at the sky to talk to you." As she said that, she smiled the most charming smile.

"May I say that you are very cute without it being considered the most terrible kind of flirting?"

"Isn't it flirting?"

"Sure it is," I answered, and I was delighted to see that my awkward effort was rewarded with a smile. Maybe there was hope. We promised each other that we would certainly be there for the next meeting and we parted.

Indeed, everybody showed up for the next meeting, including my spider. We started with some theory followed by another meditation. Again, I could see no connection between the meditation and the spider, but this time I really managed to forget the need to stop thinking, and as a result, I had a real complicated fantasy that included a wasp and a mosquito, but no spider.

"It's a bit like dreaming, this meditation. In both cases we see stuff from the subconscious, don't we?"

"Yes, you're right. Are your dreams as elaborate as your meditation visions? You have a wild imagination, Adam." I told Emilia that I often had long and elaborate dreams, like a movie.

"Shall we continue to discuss your problem in this forum, or would you prefer to talk in private?"

"No, it's OK."

"I was thinking: have you ever encountered anything similar to this spider?" I didn't quite know what to say because I felt so stupid. I had had other spider experiences before and why the fuck hadn't I told Emilia or the psychiatrist? That is a very serious case of denial.

"Adam?"

"Yeah, I had something, not the same as now, though."

"Would you like to tell us about it?"

I felt kind of silly, like a little kid whose nanny is trying to make him tell her where he got all this mud on his shoes. Anyway, the story goes like this: About ten years ago, I had a weird and disgusting dream.

In my dream I saw a sink and in the drain there was a rotten mushroom. From underneath the mushroom, particularly ugly cockroaches came crawling out of the sewer into the sink. I had no idea what that meant, but I woke up feeling terribly nauseous. It wasn't just the obnoxious image I had in my head. There was a kind of gloomy atmosphere in this dream and I was absolutely sure there was something on my bed. The time was three a.m. I got up terrified and indeed, on the sheet, right by the pillow, stood a huge black spider. I picked up the pillow and bashed it on the bed and everything on it just flew on to the floor. Of course, there was no spider and it took me a while to realize that. That was my first spider, and it was kind enough to disappear just seconds after it showed up.

That spider, or its brother perhaps, visited me twice more. The second time was in 1995. There was an earthquake not far from Eilat and it was felt in Tel Aviv. I woke up at 5:45 in the morning and everything was shaking – the bed, the lamp – it was pretty scary and lasted a few seconds. When the world stopped moving, I looked at the wall and there it was, my good old black spider friend, dropped by for a visit. This time I was ready for it. I took a deep breath, concentrated and looked at the wall and after a few seconds, it vanished.

The third spider came about three years later. It was quite similar to the second time, but without the earthquake.

What would they think of me now, I wondered as I looked at Emilia. The spider had left her nose and was now sitting on top of her head or, should I say, on the crown chakra, which is supposed to be our antenna for the reception of spiritual energies and arachnoidal energies as well, it would seem.

"Interesting." Emilia said. I guess she was right. "And you're saying that the first time you woke up from a dream about insects, you saw a spider?"

"Yeah."

"And the other times, did you dream about insects or something related to spiders as well?"

"I guess it was in the middle of a dream, but I don't think it was about insects. Is it important?"

"I'm not sure, I have to think about that. It seems that the first time you saw a spider, the hallucination continued directly from the dream, doesn't it?"

"Maybe it sounds like it, but I have to say again, when I saw the spider, I was completely awake and I was totally sure that there was a real spider on my bed. It wasn't a dream, and now it's not a dream either, it's something else."

"Yes. I got that." Anna and I left Emilia's apartment together again and after we exchanged jokes and pleasantries, I asked:

"Say, would you like to go have a cup of coffee or something?"

"In principle, yeah, I was kind of hoping you'd suggest that. I've never been out with such a tall guy – I wonder what it would be like to... Well, never mind, we'll discuss it another time." I laughed.

"I have other advantages besides being tall: With me, you have a lot more chance of running into supernatural phenomena."

"You're right, that's also very important. I'm not sure if it's a good idea to go out together before the course ends, or maybe it doesn't matter. What do you think? I have to think about it."

"Listen, there's no pressure." Actually I had a burning desire to grab her chubby thighs, move those golden curls from her forehead with my nose, and give that white neck a very serious bite. Unfortunately, pressure to sexual attraction is like red chili sauce to pecan pie – they just don't mix very well. At the next meeting, after we finished the meditation, Emilia announced:

"I have thought a great deal about your problem and I think I may have come up with something. Maybe I can solve your problem."

"Really?"

Well, I guess Madame Chakra's moment of truth had come.

"I have a theory. When you dream, you see pictures, right?"

"Yeah, sure."

"But the source of those pictures is not your eyes, right?"

"Not my eyes," I repeated, not quite comprehending what she was trying to say.

"Your eyes are closed when you dream, right?"

"Yeah, I understand what you're saying; it's like having a movie injected directly into your brain. Gee, I never thought about that. Where do the pictures come from?"

"There are many sources of energy, not just the light we see with our eyes. It's quite clear that this energy comes from the subconscious, that place we try to reach when we meditate."

"I guess a scientist would say that when we see, the electrical signals that create the pictures come from our eyes, and when we dream, they are created in some mysterious compartment of our brain. Anyway, how does that help me?"

"Well, you saw your first spider when you woke up from a dream, and there were insects in your dream, right?"

"Uh-huh."

"So, you were dreaming and this visual energy reached you from wherever it came from, and then you woke up, but somehow you continued to get this energy, which usually stops when we wake up..."

"Emilia, you're a genius! So a few seconds after I woke up, the place in my brain that's responsible for the interpretation of this information received information from two sources, and I saw the real bed and the dream spider at the same time. But wait a minute, how does it explain the spider I'm seeing right now?"

"I believe that if we explained the first spider, we are pretty close to explaining this spider. I guess you already had the energetic confusion in you, and that mushroom intensified it somehow. What we should do now is separate and channel the two kinds of energies to where they belong – vision for the day and dream energy for sleeping hours."

"Do you think it will work?"

"I hope so, but I'm not sure. I've never solved a problem like this."

And so, in the following week, I visited Emilia's apartment on a daily basis for therapy sessions. I lay on her therapy bed and closed my eyes, and Emilia told me a story about my dream energy undergoing a rough journey through a variety of chakras until it returned to its natural habitat of sleeping time and with it, my blue spider.

Miraculously, even though I don't believe that chakras exist, it worked. It took a few days. I felt intense heat in my head after the first sessions, but during our sixth session, I got up from the bed and the spider was gone. When I left her apartment, I was in a great mood and tried to reconcile this experience with my most basic beliefs about this world. I didn't convert to spirituality, I still didn't believe in chakras and spiritual energy, but Emilia with her wisdom and intuition understood my problem far better then any psychiatrist could. So she felt a need to involve chakras and spiritual stuff in it. So what? I was walking joyfully to my car when suddenly I saw something strange flying around me. No. That can't be! About twelve inches from my nose flew an orange mosquito. I lost all control of myself.

"Get the fuck out of here, you piece of orange shit," I screamed, waving my hands frantically. People passing by looked at me as if I'd gone totally nuts, and I guess they were right.

The mosquito kept hovering and buzzing near my face, and I clapped my hands in an attempt to kill it. I missed it and it gave me an offended look: "Is that how things are between us? Very well. That cute little blonde girl you desire, you can forget about her!" It disappeared, and I have never seen either it or Anna again.

Yom Kippur (The Day of Atonement)

To fast or not to fast? That supposedly was the dilemma Ben had to deal with every Yom Kippur since he had passed the age of fifteen and not eating and drinking for twenty-five hours no longer posed a challenge. In any one of those years, except for once when he felt particularly guilty, the conclusion was the same: he was too lazy and too hungry, and besides, he had an ideological excuse: it was ridiculous that one day without food and water should make him feel better about himself. It's like those Catholics confessing their sins in return for immediate redemption. Having solved the religious dilemma, he still had to deal with a more practical one – where he should spend this Yom Kippur. This year, the question was far more complicated, for another issue was at stake: What should he do about Iris? Ben and Iris had met almost a year before. The match had been made by his best friend Ron, which added an extra measure of embarrassment to the possibility of breaking up with her. Already during their first meeting, Ben felt that he was extremely attracted to her, but was also quite sure that whatever kind of relationship he would have with her wouldn't last long. Iris was a large girl, not the kind he usually fancied. She was incredibly feminine, she had big beautiful round breasts, very broad hips, and behind them an extraordinarily big and round ass. The first time she hugged him, Ben emitted a strange and unprecedented moan of pleasure that caught him by surprise and embarrassed him terribly. After a first phone call that was quite standard, they decided to meet at nine p.m. on the west corner of State Square, quite close to his apartment on Jabotinsky Street, and sit in one of the cafés around the square. It was mid-October and contrary to the weather forecast, a heavy shower began not long before nine p.m. A few minutes after nine, Ben went down to the street to look for her. She wasn't there and he fled home from the storm. Some thirty minutes later, the intercom buzzed, and two minutes after that Iris entered his apartment, all wet and sneezing. Ben apologized, made her some hot tea, and suggested that she take a shower and use his bathrobe, repeatedly stressing that this was a very innocent offer. From the minute she got out of the shower, they found it very hard to communicate.

"Would you like some more tea?" Ben wasn't sure if he was trying to be kind or just get over his embarrassment.

"I don't know. I guess I had enough of this rain." As if a cup of tea and a dress soaked with rainwater were acceptable substitutes. Only later did it occur to him that both of them were extremely sexually aroused, which made conversing a lot more difficult for both of them, and that maybe he hadn't made much sense, either.

When Iris came out of the shower, Ben realized how much he was attracted to her. Before that, there had been great embarrassment, and her red face and coughs and sneezes had also helped him to suppress his feeling. The shower helped her regain her strength. She wore his big bathrobe carelessly, exposing much of her ample breasts, and it seemed to Ben that it would soon slip off, leaving her completely naked.

"Are you sure you're OK with that robe? I didn't mean to embarrass you," he said, very embarrassed. What followed seemed to Ben unbelievably banal.

After a short conversation that didn't make any sense at all, Iris sat on his bed and said that her neck was a bit tense and could he give her a massage. Ben accepted the challenge and began kneading her neck and shoulders. He was extremely awkward since he found it very difficult to concentrate. The inner side of her thighs wasn't covered, the big breasts seemed about to burst out of the robe, and Ben's main concern was to keep his erect dick inside his trousers away from her back. Iris began to utter moans of pleasure and Ben became very excited because he hadn't slept with a woman for over a month and it seemed that this annoyingly wet evening would unexpectedly provide sex. He obviously didn't realize that in one year he and Iris would still be together and that he would be contemplating marriage. When there was no longer any doubt that Iris wanted him, Ben made the bold move of excitedly slipping his hand down her right breast. Iris looked at him with a supposedly surprised look on her face and opened the robe, which slipped down, exposing her perfect breasts and tummy and her pubic hair and sumptuous thighs and chubby legs. Ben moved to face her and rested his flannel-covered belly on her bare belly, his head between her breasts. She took off his shirt and slid her fingers along his spine, which made him utter the strange cry of pleasure that sounded as if it had come out of someone else's throat and surprised him so. On their second date, they went to see the movie, *Catch Me If You Can*, with Leonardo de Caprio. Ben loved it and was quite surprised when fifteen minutes into the movie Iris laid her head on his shoulder and announced that she was going to sleep. He was annoyed both because it seemed unintelligent and inappropriate and because it seemed to him like a manifestation of intimacy he thought they didn't share yet, in spite of the great sex they had had. She was taking this liberty without even asking first.

Her head lay like a strange and unwanted object on his shoulder, but later he softened, put his arm around her, and adjusted to the new reality.

After the movie, they walked to his apartment. Iris stopped at the very colorful window of a souvenir store and she said it was "exhalarating" – thus committing two offenses: using an inappropriate word and mispronouncing it, which always seemed to Ben to be the ultimate proof of stupidity. All the way to his apartment he phrased and rephrased in his mind the lines he would use upon arrival: She was wonderful and it wasn't her and they didn't exactly fit and so on and so forth, but he desperately wanted to continue sleeping with her because no woman had ever caused him such pleasure. So it was that he didn't say any of the above – maybe because five seconds after entering his apartment they were already naked.

During their first month together, he felt embarrassed by her at each and every meeting and wanted to tell her that they had no future together. He spent maybe half of their time together agonizing about the misery he would cause her because he already liked her a lot, and every time he postponed the unpleasant task, he was increasing the pain for both of them. After a month, he suddenly realized that she was good for him and the double relationship evolving with Mali and Ron, the matchmakers, was very pleasant.

Ben discovered a whole new world through Iris, and after a few months with her, he decided that he had previously been a dull person who didn't know the true pleasures of living. She taught him to smoke grass and prepare a joint, they went clubbing together, and she took him on outdoor trips on weekends an activity he had discussed thoroughly before meeting her, but he had always remained on the theoretical level and she had greatly increased his knowledge of the different varieties of sex.

Still, Ben didn't feel at ease in this relationship, mainly because he was afraid she wasn't smart enough for him. She continued to embarrass him in public with all sorts of silly remarks. The first time he brought her to meet his parents, she told his dad, who was a professor of astrophysics and specialized in cosmology:

"You should be able to tell us, I am a Scorpio and Ben is a Gemini, does that fit?" Somehow the "astro" and "logy" got joined together and Ben wanted to vanish from the face of the earth. His dad was actually more forgiving and gave Iris quite a long lecture on what astrophysics was and why it shouldn't under any circumstances be confused with astrology. Ron also told him that her lack of knowledge in physics didn't prevent her from being an excellent social worker and a wonderful human being. Ben agreed, but still, it bugged him, and for at least three months he came out with all sorts of excuses to avoid going to his parents. But in spite of the doubts, they stayed together. Iris would sometimes tell him to lighten up and enjoy life, which annoyed him, but that was an excellent excuse to continue this relationship and not worry too much about the future.

And so, Ben found himself walking to Iris's place just before the beginning of the Yom Kippur fast with a bagful of DVDs and some deli food hidden under a towel. (She kept telling him that they should live together and he kept postponing it with a variety of excuses.)

About two hours after the fast commenced, they had a delicious meal. Later they watched the movie *Birdy* with the young Nicholas Cage, and then it was time for the most Yom Kippurish activity of all: walking the traffic-free streets, mainly in the middle of the road. They walked hand in hand, setting out for Namir Road, which was filled with pedestrians and bicycles. There was something so calming about this secular Yom Kippur atmosphere.

They went along the Halacha Bridge to cross the Ayalon Highway toward Bialik Street in Ramat Gan, where they saw more and more skullcap-covered heads of religious men and modestly dressed young women. At the junction of Bialik and Abba Hillel, there was a very big crowd. "I wonder why there are so many people at this particular junction," said Ben.

"I don't know."

"It looks like an open synagogue."

"It's funny that there are so many happy people in the streets on Yom Kippur of all days; it's like a big wedding. I hope there'll be as many happy people at our wedding."

Ben wasn't sure how to respond. He was 27 and Iris was only 24 and so far he seemed to have successfully avoided any serious discussion about their future. Actually he had had many such discussions, but they had all taken place within the safe confines of his mind. Now she was telling him quite casually that she wanted to get married. He considered saying something neutral such as "Uh-huh" or "I see." Then he considered changing the subject altogether by diverting her attention to an appallingly fat woman who passed by them. Finally he blurted out something incoherent.

"What did you say?"

"No, I mean, nothing."

"You were saying something."

"I don't know."

"You don't know what?"

"Somehow, I'm not really sure we'll get married." Oops, what did he just say? Was it a good idea to say that? There could be serious repercussions and he certainly hadn't planned things like that – not on that day, anyway. On the other hand, that may have been his most honest moment in the whole relationship.

"You're not sure, or you're sure it won't happen?"

Ben stood silently and tried to think. This crisis was not what he wanted right now, so what was he doing? On the other hand, maybe it was time to make choices. How long can you stay with someone you know you will never marry?

"Ben?" He remained silent.

"I think I got the point," Iris said, her voice trembling, as a tear ran down her cheek. Ben raised his hand to caress and wipe her cheek, but she removed it.

"I really love you and I thought that..." She began to cry, but immediately took out a handkerchief, wiped her face and regained her self-control. Ben knew exactly what she was about to say because she had already said it so many times. Iris had had many boyfriends and they had all enjoyed her tremendously and then dumped her after a few months, claiming that they couldn't live with all her nonsense. With Ben she finally thought she had found someone who accepted her as she was.

"I think it's time to say goodbye."

"Now?" Ben was truly shocked even though it was no surprise, of course.

"I want to be alone." She kissed his cheek and started walking back to Tel Aviv. Ben considered chasing after her and begging for his life, but he had no idea what he wanted and he remained frozen. He started walking along Bialik Street toward Ramat Gan and tried to collect his thoughts.

Many couples were walking with their arms around each other near him and he suddenly found it a bit hard to breathe. What had he done? He loved Iris and now he was left all by himself. He thought about Iris walking home alone crying and he also wanted to cry.

He continued walking and lost all sense of time and direction. He took a turn from the main street away from the happy crowd and then made another turn; he wasn't quite sure where he was. He looked around him and saw that he was all alone on an unfamiliar street. Suddenly he heard someone whispering. He inspected his surroundings trying to find the name of the street. It was a street of big individual houses. He was standing by a big fence and the voices seemed to be coming from above the fence, probably from the yard of one of the houses. He tried to make out what they were saying, but he only heard fragments of sentences. Their accent sounded Yemenite or something similar. One of them was probably thirty-five, maybe more, the other was young, perhaps twenty. Ben was almost sure he heard the words "Ashkenazi whore" (Ashkenazis are Jews of East European origin) and he smiled. What a strange Yom Kippur. Then a few wards were said about the Jewish fast and about giving charity to the poor. Then there was silence and Ben heard what sounded to him like they were rummaging through a bag. "OK, in we go." Ben heard the order given by the older guy very clearly. Could they be breaking into the house? On the other hand, maybe they owned the house – was he a racist? Was their accent enough for him to assume that they were burglars? But there was something about the way they were whispering and the urgent tone of the words that suggested that a crime was being committed rather than two innocent guys chilling out in their yard.

What should he do? He took a few steps back from the fence. A few yards away there were steps down from the yard to the sidewalk. He walked toward the steps and from there he could see a part of the house that looked dark, but the moon was up in the sky and he managed to see quite clearly. He could see a part of the door and he figured that had they entered through the door, he would probably have heard it,

and they would have turned on the light. But this was Yom Kippur, and that could explain the darkness. Ben tried to pick up a clue about what was going on in the house, but there was nothing. He hesitated, went toward the steps and backed away, then walked to the steps again and climbed up three of them to improve his angle of vision of the house, but he saw nothing. He could see the entire front of the house now, but he saw no one. It was a nice house. In the front there was a nicely mowed lawn – his eyes were at the level of the lawn – and there was something elegant and restrained about it that suggested wealth in spite of the simplicity of the house: a tiled roof, a brick façade and two big windows. But along the door there was a colorful, expensive-looking stained-glass panel illuminated by a small spotlight, and the path leading to the door was made of small, neatly arranged mosaic stones.

He went down the three steps back to the sidewalk and felt like a soldier returning home from enemy territory. Even this little peek at the house had strained his nerves and he was dripping with sweat. Maybe there was a way to check out what was happening behind the house. Maybe he should just go to the door and knock. That was truly a stroke of genius; he was alarmed by the stupidity of his own ideas. Ben walked along the fence and saw that between this house and the next, there was a gap through which a path led somewhere inside. He couldn't tell where the path led to – another row of houses perhaps? But he thought that by taking the path he would be able to get behind the house and see what was happening.

He stood by the gap, his heart pounding like crazy. He looked around anxiously. If people saw him standing like this, they might think that he was the offender here, but the street was empty. He took a step on to the path and froze. This whole thing was probably a figment of his imagination. Supposing there was a crime taking place, so what?

These millionaires living here, did they care about him, would they risk a hair of their heads to help him? They lived their rich lives and didn't give a shit about anything; what business was it of his if their house was broken into? Big drops of sweat were running down his forehead and he wiped them with his sleeves and tried to take a deep breath, but the air seemed to be stuck somewhere in his throat and only a small dose of oxygen reached his chest. He tried to regain his breath. He was still no more than a yard from the main street. He cleared his throat and coughed a little and thought, What an idiot, making so much noise.

If there was anyone there, they could hear him from miles away. He had barely finished this thought when he heard a noise nearby and his head was banged against the fence. He didn't lose consciousness, but he felt a little dizzy. His neck hurt terribly and it took him a few seconds to realize that a big hand was grasping him by the neck and almost strangling him. Whoever it was began to drag him along the fence away from the main street, occasionally muttering, "You son of a bitch!" and banging his head against the wall again and again. Ben wanted to cry, but he couldn't because of the hand that was almost strangling him. After a few more seconds, which seemed like an eternity, they reached the back of the house and Ben heard the older guy say:

"Well, well, well, what have we here?"

"Jackie, I caught this son of a bitch near the house, spying on us, the motherfucker!" and again, Ben's head was bashed against the wall.

"Awww, I didn't see anything, what do you want from me?" He was in a state of complete panic, but as he pronounced the words, he realized that this wasn't the most brilliant thing to say.

"You lying motherfucker, do you think we're stupid? Jackie, all these Ashkenazi motherfuckers think we're all suckers!" And again, Ben was hit in the head. Ben thought his head wouldn't stand much more of it.

"I won't tell anybody... I... I'm a coward, there's not a chance that I'd go to the police, I... I mean... I just want to continue my life, I wouldn't risk my life tipping off the police." He was on the verge of tears and his voice broke a few times in mid-sentence.

"Sure, that's what you say now, but in the police station, we won't be there to scare your miserable little ass, right?" Ben got kicked in his leg, his head was pressed against the wall, and his vision was blurred. He couldn't see it, but he could practically sense Mendy, the young one moving his hand along his throat and he thought how stupid it would be to die in this ugly backyard because of some implausible chain of events. Why did Iris have to talk about weddings today of all days? This somewhat philosophical thought made him a little calmer and he tried to use this temporary composure to say something.

"Look, I speak many languages, and in the army they wanted to put me in Intelligence..."

"What's that shit you're saying now?"

"Sssh…" Jackie calmed him down.

"What are you saying?" There was something soothing in his voice now and Ben tried to make the point from start to finish.

"I said that they wanted to take me into Intelligence, but I didn't want it because I knew that if I were ever captured, I'd break instantly. I'm telling you, there's no chance I'll go to the police. Let me go and you'll never hear of me again." Ben was pleased with his relative calm; his voice was less whiny now. Then Mendy said:

"Jackie, we can't let the son of a bitch go to the police." There was a pause of a few seconds that seemed like eternity, and then Jackie spoke.

"You know? I went to the synagogue today, spoke some with the rabbi, gave some money to charity, asked for a blessing, so we would have no troubles with the wife and kids, you know?"

"Uh-huh."

"It's Yom Kippur today, we're both fasting. Have you no fear?" Ben was flooded with a wave of relief.

"So what are you saying? We let the sucker go and God Almighty will keep his mouth shut?"

"Look, I can see that… what's your name?"

"What? Ben, my name is Ben."

"Ben here speaks languages and he must be a pretty smart guy and he knows that I never forget a face, and if he fucks with us, he'll be in deep shit and his life will be very short, right, Ben?"

"Yeah, yeah, sure."

"Ben, do you have any ID on you?"

"What?"

"ID, do you have some ID on you?" Luckily, Ben had his driving license on him. He took it out of his pocket and it was taken away.

"So, we know exactly who you are now, we can find you very easily. Do you understand that?"

"Yes." They whispered. Ben's head was still pressed against the wall, but Mendy's grip was a little more relaxed now.

"Ben, we're walking with you to the main street, you got that?" He tried to respond, but no sound came out.

"What are you saying?"

"Yeah, yeah." His head was held two feet from the ground. Jackie went to check if the street was clean and came back.

"OK, we're out of here. Ben?" he said smirking.

It seemed that he derived great pleasure from wielding control over other people and maybe even greater pleasure from this divine grace he was now administering.

"Yeah?"

"You will now count to one hundred and only then will you take your head away from this wall, right?"

"Uh-huh."

"And then you're out of here like a rocket. If you go to the police, we will know about it and we will find you. You will remember who gave you your life, right?" Somewhere in the back of his mind, he had the notion to amuse them by saying "I think it was my mother," but they probably wouldn't find it so funny.

"Yeah, you have nothing to worry about, I'll never tell anyone about this." Ben felt extremely relieved when the big hand let go of his neck. There was a slight tap on his shoulder.

"May you be inscribed in the book of life, Ben. No less than one hundred, yeah? Goodbye, Ben."

Ben heard them moving quickly away. He counted to one hundred as ordered and only then did he open his eyes and sigh in relief. He looked around him and saw no trace of them, and looked at his watch and was amazed to discover that only thirty minutes had passed since he and Iris had broken up. That event seemed to him like a faint memory. His forehead and neck hurt terribly, but there was no bleeding. He felt his leg and there was a slight swelling over his right ankle. He walked a few steps and it wasn't so bad. He should go to Iris. But he had just broken up with her, or was it the other way around? His toilet bag was at her place. He checked his pockets and found his keys inside, thank God! What was he to do now? Maybe he should go into this house and check if anybody needed help there.

But he had told them that he would be out of there – "like a rocket," Jackie had said, and what if they were still waiting somewhere, checking on him? This was insane! He could call the police – maybe the two of them were not yet too far away, and he knew their names! He could help the police get the bastards! The memory of the harsh treatment he had suffered crept in immediately, however; they could kill him very easily and they had his personal data! The mere thought of going to the police or doing anything else that might involve him with those two again filled him with terror: he should forget he ever saw them. Anyway the house was empty, he could tell that it was empty!

The spotlight in the entrance was still on and maybe another little light inside. But no! If there were people recovering from an armed robbery, surely he would hear or see something suggesting that they were there.

What was done was done, and he wouldn't help anyone by ruining his own life. After walking for a little more than thirty minutes, he got home, and only when he collapsed into his living-room armchair did he realize how exhausted he was. He napped for a few minutes and then went to the bathroom and looked in the mirror. In the middle of his forehead, there was a red ugly bulge. What was he to do now? Maybe call Iris and tell her about it? He really needed some love and support, but he didn't feel he was up to dealing with the Iris issue. Maybe he should call Ron? And tell him what? The truth perhaps? But that was a terrible stain; he had behaved like such a coward! He shouldn't tell anyone! Ever! Should he talk to Ron, they would be obliged to reach the conclusion that the only decent thing to do was to go to the police as soon as possible and that would be extremely stupid! It was one thing if he had reported it immediately after the event, but now? He would look like a complete coward and for what? He should keep his mouth shut! Why should he be responsible for this mess?

Just because he ran into those ugly thugs by mistake? On the other hand, he had seen what he had seen and there was no denying that; he would always know the truth.

Ben suddenly remembered all sorts of stories he'd heard about the Holocaust. In Jewish history, there were lots of cases of people who pretended to be ignorant. Was he any better? Surely the Nazi thugs were a lot more scary then these two superstitious little criminals, and the threat of being sent to the Russian front or dying under torture by the Gestapo was infinitely more frightening. What should he tell Ron and other people he'd meet the next day? He could just say that he was mugged; he didn't see anything, so there was no point going to the police. Yeah, that's the solution!

Ben realized that he felt bad not just because of physical pain, but because he was humiliated. For five minutes, he had been completely at their mercy, and he had felt like a sheep about to be slaughtered. He would have done anything, betrayed anyone, so they would leave him alone. Maybe he should go to the police just so he could regain his self-respect. But the mere thought was enough to make it hard to breathe; the memory of the big hand pounding his head against the wall was extremely vivid and they had his name and ID number! Any second-rate detective could find him based on that. He should erase this episode from his memory! Having your home broken into is pretty nasty, but he should put this into proportion. Nobody had died here; this event had nothing to do with the Holocaust, and it was better for some one else's home to be broken into than for Ben to be hunted like an animal for the rest of his life. But what about the future crimes of those two? They were very dangerous and they would surely have killed him if it hadn't been Yom Kippur. Wasn't he obliged to try to prevent them from killing others? But no! Ben felt enraged by the mere thought. There were all sorts of stupid nice guys in this world willing to sacrifice themselves for others.

Ben was not one of them, and anyway, he wasn't responsible for any crime other than the one he had witnessed, and he could live with that in order to live a quiet life: That was the rational choice even if he had some stupid impulse to be a hero.

Ben relaxed a little and suddenly noticed that he was terribly hungry and thirsty. He turned on the faucet and drank some water, but he didn't eat, and when on the morning of Yom Kippur he decided to skip breakfast he imagined Ron mocking him:

"Ben, am I imagining things or have you actually decided to fast?"

"No, not really. I'm not hungry, that's all, and I still have a terrible headache from yesterday."

But he did observe the remainder of the Yom Kippur fast with the exception of some water he allowed himself on account of his injury. As the day passed, the whole incident seemed more and more like some surrealistic dream. When the fast ended at five o'clock, he was desperately hungry. He opened the fridge to find it quite empty – all the food he had from Yom Kippur was with Iris. He found one container of cream cheese and he took a box of Pringles, which he dipped in the cheese. A few minutes later, the Pringles were gone. Where did he get this stupid idea to stop eating because two ugly criminals had nearly beaten him to death and then almost decided to kill him? In the next few days, Ben couldn't stop thinking about this event. It was very difficult to concentrate on his work, and two days later, he decided to return to the scene of the crime and try to find out what had happened there. He looked at the map and concluded that it had taken place in McDonald Street, close to the Diamond Exchange district. The second evening after Yom Kippur, Ben drove from work to Bialik Street, parked his car not far from the entrance to McDonald Street, and started walking. He looked around, trying to make sure that he really was in the right street.

The last time he had been here it was quite dark and the trauma also made it more difficult to remember. It was a street of nice houses and that certainly fit. There weren't too many people around and Ben still feared that his attackers were hiding somewhere, waiting for him, even though he knew it was a ridiculous fear. He passed by a police car, continued to walk a few more meters and stopped. He went back, passed by two houses, and saw a gap in the wall to his left where a little path led inside. Was that it? The police car was parked in front of the house and Ben crossed the street to the other side so he could see the house. There was no doubt; that was it. There was a man in the police car and the car door was open toward the stairs leading to the house. Ben wanted to ask the policeman what had happened there, but he just stood frozen. Oh well, he knew that a break-in had taken place, and now the police were here and that meant nothing. He decided to get the hell away from there before the policeman noticed him. Ben began walking to his car, but he was extremely anxious to find out exactly what had happened. On the way to his car he saw a woman with shopping bags entering her house.

"Excuse me?"

"Yes?"

"Do you have any idea why the police are there?"

"I'm not sure; something terrible happened there, maybe a rape or a murder or something, God help us all."

"Thank you." Ben walked away quickly.

He felt that his head was about to burst; he had this impossible hollow feeling in his head similar to a hangover, as if someone had stuck a hot iron plate in his skull. Murder, rape – what had he done? But this was partial information; he had to find out exactly what had happened. He ran to the Bialik Street and bought a newspaper in the first kiosk he found. He then ran to his car and got into it breathless and soaked in sweat. He turned on the air conditioning, rested for a minute to regain his breath, and began leafing through the paper frantically. It wasn't on the first page. He opened the paper, tearing through the pages as he looked through all the sections. After a few minutes, he found something that seemed to fit: "**The hunt for the 'Yom Kippur' murderers continues.** ...The break-in took place on McDonald Street in Ramat Gan and the police are conducting an extensive search for the murderers.

It appears that the woman was hit on the head with a blunt object and that she was still alive when the police arrived at the scene. Her condition was serious and she was proclaimed dead on arrival at Ichilov Hospital in Tel Aviv. ...jewelry was taken... her husband, who was not at home, was notified..." Ben felt as if he were suffocating. He opened the car windows, but that was not enough. As he tried to breathe, he only felt that he wanted to run away, but there was nowhere to go. He stumbled out of the car, bent down and puked. What had he done? That was impossible. He was still down on the ground, holding his head in his hands four inches from the sidewalk, the sour stench of puke filling his nostrils.

"Sir, are you OK?" Ben looked up and saw a woman about his age looking at him with empathetic eyes.

"Yeah, yeah, I'm sorry." Somehow, the shame caused by the spectacle he had made of himself brought him back to his senses. He stood up dizzy and got into the car, the stench still reaching his nostrils through the open window. A long list of liberal arguments that he would expound to anyone who would listen swirled around in his head: Israel, he would say, was not a serious country. Most of the mess originated from the lack of awareness of the importance of cooperating with the system. In a normal Western state, people paid their taxes because they understood that with no taxes, there was no education, no health, and so on.

In Israel, too small a portion of the population realized that, and it appeared that those who did understand didn't have the balls to do the right thing. The more he thought, the less he could find any difference between himself and those Germans who had just stood by and done nothing. True, his cowardice had caused one death and theirs had caused millions, but the difference was only in quantity.

He looked in the mirror and saw that his lips were still covered with little bits of puke.

He wiped his mouth, sat staring into space for another minute, and drove home. When he entered his apartment, he washed his face, took off all his clothes and lay naked and exhausted on the bed. What had he done? He tried to recreate in his mind that terrible moment when he had sat on the sidewalk by the house trying to figure out what to do, as if he could now take a different course of action and change what had happened. What had he been thinking? As he was walking home, and the murderers were already miles away, there was a woman dying on the floor of the house and maybe he could have saved her. He hadn't even checked. While he was examining those minor wounds he had sustained, a woman was bleeding on the floor a few yards from him. He could have taken a look, just to make sure. He could have called for an ambulance anonymously – there were many decent courses of action that wouldn't have put him at risk at all. But he hadn't bother to think, he just ran away like... like the coward he really was.

Ben remembered a scene from *Saving Private Ryan*: Apphaum, the platoon interpreter, is lying behind a small mound. On the other side, five Germans are firing at his buddies. He can surprise the Germans, kill some of them, and save some of his friends. But will he kill all the Germans and what will they do to him should he fail? Ben watched this DVD and he replayed that scene over and over again.

Each time he could feel Apphaum's horror and identify with it, and each time it seemed that now Apphaum would shoot the enemy and save his friends. Whenever he had watched this previously, he had wondered what he would do. Would he choose the cowardly option that made Apphaum the only survivor of his platoon? It seemed that now he had received the answer. He got up and went to the mirror: he looked beaten, pathetic. What a worthless loser; how could he live with himself? He felt a wave of nausea and a shortness of breath again; he coughed harshly and walked shakily to the living room. He could still call the police, he thought. He hadn't prevented the murder, but he could help get the murderers. But what would he tell them? That he could have prevented a murder, but hadn't? Other than ruining his life, it would achieve nothing, he thought, and then, as if struck by lightning, he knew what he should do, and a wave of relief swept over him: he had ruined the life of one woman; he would make another woman happy.

"Hello, Iris?" Ben didn't know what to expect.

"Ben?"

"Yeah."

"How are you?" Unsurprisingly, her voice was cold.

"I'm OK, more or less. After we went our separate ways on Yom Kippur," (he desperately wanted to avoid the term "broke up") "some nut head hit me over the head with a big stick and I have a big ugly wound, but I'm OK."

"Oh my God, are you sure you're OK?"

"Yeah. I..."

"Yeah?"

"Could you come over?" There was silence for maybe thirty seconds and then she said:

"OK, but that doesn't change anything between us, does it?"

"Ahh…"

"Yeah?" Her tone of voice changed dramatically. Ben took a deep breath; he knew that the words he was about to say would have a profound impact on his life. Ben had always made it a rule not to make decisions under pressure. He would always wait until he had regained his calm, and now he was making the most important of decisions in the middle of the storm. But he needed to atone immediately for what he had done, or rather, for what he hadn't done. He needed to regain his faith in his humanity or he would go crazy.

"I had some time to think during Yom Kippur and I reached some conclusions. We need to talk."

"I'll be right over." She hung up and Ben knew that that was it; nothing specific had been said, but both of them knew exactly what he had just said, and by denying it now, he would lose whatever was left of his self-respect.

The wedding was set for six months later. It was mid-spring, the weather was wonderful, and Ben and Iris sat huddled in the back seat of the limousine taking them to the wedding gardens where they would get married.

"Are you happy?"

"Yes, I'm happy," he said, and kissed her on her lips.

Iris would ask this question often and Ben would always give the same answer. He wondered what it sounded like. It wasn't exactly a lie; Ben really loved Iris and he decided that marrying her was the only way to find some peace and maintain a sense of value, but he wasn't truly happy.

"Look, it's six already. The huppa is supposed to take place in thirty minutes and we're stuck in this traffic jam. It's terrible."

"Don't worry, we'll make it. Zion, could you turn on the radio? I want to listen to the news."

"What do you need that for? We're getting married and all he cares about is the news," she said with a big smile on her face.

They heard a commercial for dairy products.

"Sorry, I guess we missed the news."

"Oh well, never mind."

"I did hear that there's going to be a municipal strike, so you can expect big piles of garbage for your honeymoon."

"We're going to Greece," they shouted together and smiled.

"What else?"

"Ah, you remember that terrible business in Ramat Gan six months ago? That lawyer who bled her brains out on her living-room floor?"

"Zion, will you cut that crap?" Iris said angrily, and Zion apologized humbly. Ben thought he was about to puke.

"Well? What did you hear about that?"

"I don't think the lady wants to hear that."

"Please, just tell me what you heard," Ben begged.

"Honey, are you OK?"

"Yeah, I just want to hear the story."

"Alma Rosenzweig, that was her name, poor thing. She was loaded, a real multi-millionairess. Anyway, they had been sure – well, you know that it happened on Yom Kippur and there was a break-in and the police were sure that it was the burglars. It appears now that it was her husband; he suspected her of cheating on him or something fucked up like that, so he hit her with a baseball bat."

Ben felt dizzy and his mind was racing – it wasn't them, which meant it wasn't him! And what did that mean? As their wedding drew nearer and the humiliating memory faded somewhat, he had often wondered if marrying Iris was really the right choice. On the other hand, this delightful piece of news didn't turn him into a better human being. He looked at Iris joyfully anticipating their wedding while he wasn't sure he wanted to be there any more. Atoning for your crimes was a terrible reason to get married he had realized long ago. But could he abandon her now? That would be terrible; he couldn't do that to her. But could he do this to himself? Ben realized that there was nothing in the world that could make him tell her now, on the way to their wedding, that he had changed his mind. He looked out the window at the traffic jam gradually opening up.

The limousine began to accelerate along the path of no return leading to the wedding he wasn't sure he wanted to attend.

"Honey, are you OK? You look a little worried."

Ben looked at Iris sadly.

"Yeah, it's just that I'm so excited."

Six thirty in the morning. I tried to remember what time I had gone to sleep – maybe three thirty, maybe four a.m., I wasn't sure. I needed more sleep, but for some reason, I couldn't fall asleep. I sat on the bad and yawned. The room wasn't completely dark. The shutters were closed, but light came through the open door. I took the alarm clock and examined it closely. There was no doubt, it was six thirty in the morning, and in spite of the fatigue, I knew that for me, this night was over.

I got up, walked out of the room and looked around. Where the hell was I? I was in a small foyer in an unfamiliar apartment. On the floor lay an elegant reddish carpet, the ceiling was wood-paneled, in the corner stood a flowerpot on a round copper stand, and on the wall facing the door there was a big mirror.

I entered the living room, which also looked very expensive and tastefully designed: two black leather couches, an oak bookcase, a big flat TV, and some other equipment. I looked at the books and smiled. At least I had stayed with a girl who loved books; that was nice. There were quite a few books I had read – a few detective novels by Batya Gur, lots of Graham Greenes and Herman Wouks, many science fiction books such as *The Moon is a Harsh Mistress* by Robert Heinlein, one of my all-time favorites, and *The Robot Serious* by Isaac Asimov. There were also all kinds of books by authors with Japanese names that I had never heard of – Kazuo Ishiguro, Haruki Murakami – which looked very interesting. It reminded me of Miri, the girlfriend I had after my military service: You're so morbid, she told me, you see death even in books.

She said this when we were standing in her father's library and I told her that I read around twenty books each year.

That meant that by the time I'd read a thousand books, give or take, I would die. I didn't even have enough time for the books in that one library.

The living room opened on to a big veranda with a great view of… the Mediterranean! Where was I? I looked outside and was dazzled by the sunlight. Far below stretched the promenade, full of people. Tel Aviv, I was in Tel Aviv. I lived in Jerusalem and I didn't even remember getting to Tel Aviv. I must have gotten completely drunk the previous night! But whose apartment was this?

"Is anybody home?" I shouted, but there was no response. I was going back to the foyer toward the bathroom when someone passed me by. There was something familiar about him, but I didn't recognize him. It wasn't one of my close friends, and it seemed that there was no basis in reality for my optimistic assumption that I was with a girl. This guy was about thirty-five, ten years older than me, more or less my height, balding, a very short haircut. Who could it be? I went into the kitchen: "Excuse me?" I was quite sure I would find him there, but the man seemed to have vanished! I went back to the living room, but there was no trace of him. What was I doing in his apartment anyway? I must have been so drunk that the guys put me in the nearest apartment to the bar they could find. How embarrassing!

I decided to wash my face in the kitchen; bathrooms can be sort of intimate. In the sink there were a few plates and two cups – quite clean for a Tel Aviv sink. I turned on the tap and washed my face under a powerful stream, spraying water all around me. After drying myself off with a few paper towels, I rinsed out my mouth and felt a little better.

As I was drying the floor, it hit me. I saw the sun over the sea; what time was it now? I went back to the bedroom and it was already seven o'clock, but which seven? I returned to the veranda and there was no doubt about it: the sun was hiding behind a big cloud lying low above the horizon, its contours glowing gold and white. I was looking at the sunset and the time was seven p.m., not seven a.m. I had lost a whole day! It seemed as if I had lost my orientation, as happens with jetlag. I was unable to decide whether I was tired or stupefied by too much sleep, and I felt a bit heavy, as if I had put on a few pounds. Another memory of Miri: It was right after I had returned from the big trip to the Far East. We were sitting on the Tel Aviv promenade watching the sunset and she asked:

"In all your travels, did you ever see a sunset as beautiful as this one?"

It was truly a spectacular sunset, beauty that words can't describe.

"What the fuck are you talking about? The Tel Aviv sunsets are nice, but you need a change of scenery sometimes, right?"

Now, I was suddenly saddened by my rudeness then and at other times. Why can't I be nicer? I needed some coffee!

"Is there anybody there?" I asked again loudly, but there was no reply. I decided to boil some water and maybe eat some cookies from the box I'd seen in the kitchen, even though my host was nowhere to be found. If he let me sleep in his bed (which was kind of worrying), he probably wouldn't mind my having some coffee and cookies.

I drank on the veranda. The sun had already set, the sea was a beautiful deep blue, a pleasant breeze was caressing me, and I had an urge to go out and meet the world. On the chair by his computer table lay a pile of clothes that seemed to be mine, though I wasn't totally sure. But I was in my underwear and didn't seem to have any other options. What a computer he had! A huge flat screen the likes of which I was not sure I'd ever seen.

I put on the clothes, which fit me exactly, wrote a letter of apology saying that I would be back in thirty minutes, and put it on the keyboard. I took the keys out of the keyhole, went out and locked the door behind me. I really hoped that my host wouldn't show up while I was out; that could be terribly embarrassing. Maybe he'd just gone for a chat with the neighbor and hadn't taken the key. Never mind, I'd just breathe some sea air and come back.

When I left the building, the doorman greeted me and I answered him politely. What a nice building! My host was doing pretty well. I crossed the road to the promenade, which was swarming with people! How wonderful it is to smell the sea the minute you go out of your house. If I work hard, maybe I'll also own a great apartment like that when I'm thirty-five!

I walked along the promenade for a few minutes. There were so many beautiful women in Tel Aviv! One girl, cute with black hair flowing over her shoulders, smiled at me and turned and stared at me after she had passed me by. Ah, what a beautiful evening. I passed a kiosk and decided to buy a newspaper. I searched my pocket and felt a credit card and a few notes. Was that my money? I assumed it was; it's incredible how out of it I was. I bought the paper, sat on the wall separating the promenade from the sand, and started to read. **Another deadly suicide attack!** it said in blood-red letters, and my mood was suddenly not so wonderful. **Twenty fatalities, number liable to increase! Another hundred injured, some seriously!** For some reason, I thought that the Palestinians had decided to stop those terror attacks. I folded the newspaper, having lost any desire to read it. Why did I have to buy it, anyway? I looked around me and people seemed as happy as ever.

I guess we get used to all sorts of shit; it's just a matter of time. I went back to the building and the uniformed doorman greeted me again. I went up to the fifth floor and knocked cautiously on the door. There was no answer. I guessed my rich host was still out. I went inside and yelled "Hello?"

I lifted my shirt a little bit and patted my tummy. This was weird; I really did feel heavier. Maybe it was my bladder. When was the last time I'd been to the bathroom? Only God knows how long I'd slept and how much beer I'd drunk the previous night.

Before I went to the bathroom, I stood opposite the mirror in profile and lifted my shirt again to check if I had gained any weight. My God, when did I get this fat? I turned to face the mirror and a thirty-five-year-old balding man was staring at me. Ah, you're finally back, I said, and looked back, but there was nobody there. I looked at the mirror again and suddenly my breath became short and heavy and my eyesight a little dim. I closed my eyes and tried to breathe steadily and concentrate so I wouldn't faint. When I opened my eyes again, he was still standing there, the old man. I lifted my right arm and he followed, I touched my left cheek and he did the same, refusing to stop this stupid joke. I felt my hair and screamed. Only now had my brain fully grasped what was already clear to my eyes: that was me and I'd lost my hair. My beautiful brown hair that was greased with gel had disappeared and in its place was this pathetic joke. I remembered Miri again; she used to laugh at me for using all sorts of remedies against balding. I guess none of them helped. What were those little wrinkles in my forehead?

I went to the kitchen and drank some water. So was this my apartment? I opened the door and there was my name neatly printed near the bell.

How had I gotten this luxurious apartment and why did I have to lose my hair now of all times when I had such a great condo by the beach? Who would want me now, anyway?

The newspaper! I needed the newspaper. I began to read: There was a suicide attack... Prime Minister Sharon says that there will be no negotiations under fire... Prime Minister Sharon? What in the name of God happened to Rabin? I looked at the date and it seemed ok:

October 30th, 2003. 2003???????

I continued to read. A memorial service for Yitzhak Rabin, who was murdered on November 4th, 1995, would be held in Rabin Square in a few days. In the territories and in Israel, a war called the Al Aqsa Intifada was raging.

It turned out that I hadn't lost a day, I'd lost a decade!

I went out on to the veranda – my veranda, apparently; the time was nine p.m. and the sea was covered with a thick black blanket. I climbed on to the railing and jumped.

The Lord giveth and the Lord taketh away, blessed be the name of the Lord! This strange biblical association brought an unexpected smile to my face.

"You sure are taking the bad news well. They meet every Wednesday, like a Swiss watch, from five p.m. to seven p.m."

"The Italian cooking course; I thought it might be then."

"Italian cooking?"

"Yeah, Italian cooking." In the last few years, Ella had attended a variety of cooking courses. The first time was after she read *The Kitchen* by Banana Yoshimoto. Until then, she had always complained how stuffy all sushi lovers are – "How can you eat these pieces of raw fish and praise them as if they were culinary masterpieces? It's unbelievable what people are willing to put in their mouths for the sake of impressions" – and of course, I was among the condemned sushi lovers. It turned out that literary descriptions could have an interesting affect on the taste buds. She read this rather short book in one evening after work and immediately after turning the last page asked if I felt like going out to a Japanese restaurant.

"But you hate Japanese food. You despise people who like that food, except for me, I hope." Anyway, going out for a meal at eleven thirty p.m. was crazy; we had to get up for work in the morning.

"The truth is that I don't think I've ever eaten any Japanese food, and I want to try." She showed me the Yoshimoto book and we went out to a sushi bar on Rothschild Boulevard.

Two months before, Ella had ordered an Italian cookbook through Amazon called *The Science of Cooking and the Art of Eating Well* by one

Pellegrino Artusi from the end of the nineteenth century, and then she started going to that imaginary Italian cooking course. It's a real classic, she told me. What a bitch! It really did strike me as a weird purchase! I mean, she didn't owe me any explanations; she could study Mongol BBQ without reading the biography of Genghis Khan!

It all began one day when I took her mobile phone with me by mistake – we both had the same model, but we really tried to avoid this sort of mix-up as both phones contained a whole lot of important numbers. I entered the name list and pressed W to find Martin Wolfberg, who was a client. Instead I reached Whoisit-Mobile and Whoisit-Apartment. I obviously realized what had happened, but I think it was quite understandable that I got kind of curious. Who was Whoisit? At first I was amused by my funny woman, who kept the phone number of people called Whoisit. But the more I thought it over, the more it bothered me. Who is it really? There was one way to find out. I wrote down the number, but I didn't make the call. For a few days, I went around with this number in my pocket and tried to make up my mind. Calling would be prying. It would almost be like following her and she had never given me any reason to suspect her of anything. But after a few days, when I realized that I just couldn't get this out of my mind, I decided to make the call. What could possibly happen?

The following Sunday, having parked my car by my office, I called the mobile number of Whoisit and blocked caller identification – the last thing I needed was for Whoisit to report this call to Ella.

Having keyed in the numbers, I laid the phone down and wondered one last time if I should make the call. What good would it do? Even if she was cheating on me, did I want to know? Why jeopardize the lovely life I had? We were so good together. The sex was also good and I hadn't noticed anything different lately. Ella still told me that she loved me when she came. Or maybe she didn't anymore? Suddenly I wasn't so sure. Maybe she'd stopped doing that, maybe I could no longer satisfy her. Maybe Ella faked her orgasms. What a pile of garbage was accumulating in my head! I should make the call. A strange woman would probably answer, I would hang up and that would be the end of it. So I pressed the OK button and my phone transmitted the fateful signal. Someone said hello at the other end and I was so shocked that the phone slipped from my hand and landed on the mat by the gas pedal. I picked up the phone, heard another hello, and hung up. The voice belonged to my dear childhood friend, Michael. True, I hadn't heard that voice for a few years, but I used to hear it constantly from dawn till sunset. There was no mistake here; it was Michael. I'm not sure how long I sat there in the same position, head tilted just a little bit, mouth half open, right hand stretched out holding the phone. I heard a knock on my window and that pulled me out of the trance. Sam, another lawyer stood by my car window.

"Good morning, are you coming up?"

"What? No, no, you go up, I have to make another phone call."

"OK, see you upstairs." He left me and I tried to figure out what I was going to do now. This didn't make any sense. Why did my wife have Michael's number listed as Whoisit? My suspicion that my wife was cheating on me was gradually turning into a conclusion.

"Erik, are you OK?" Sam was standing by my window again.

"What? Yeah, yeah, just a little family problem.

I might have to take the day off."

He looked at me for another moment, trying to make up his mind whether he should try to learn more about my catatonic state, but he gave up, said goodbye, and went up to the office. It was quite clear that I didn't want to work right now, even though they say that work is the best diversion. I called the office secretary and she was already prepared with my schedule. Luckily, there was nothing that couldn't be postponed that day. I wanted to feel numb; I needed to get drunk. I wasn't sure that it was pain I felt – I was so surprised that I didn't know what to feel. I thought that my life would probably never be the same ever again. But what would replace it? Divorce? Would I start dating again? It all seemed too far-fetched and I didn't want to think about it.

I drove to the Tel Aviv promenade, went into one of the bars, and asked for a Long Island ice tea, which is the best way I know to get high. The only time I truly got drunk was when I drank two of those on an empty stomach. When I got my drink, I started to think that maybe I was jumping to the wrong conclusions. There were very good grounds for suspicion but no proof yet, only circumstantial evidence. How the fuck did she know him, that's what I wanted to know. When we got married, Michael was in the States. It had been years since I last talked to him and I wasn't even sure if I had ever told her about him. Why shouldn't I just talk to her about it? But if it turned out that I was wrong, that could be terrible. The same went for talking to any friends. I could turn a non-issue into a real crisis. I had better get some reliable intelligence before taking any steps.

I drank my cocktail with a straw and after a few sips, I could feel that blessed fog creeping into my brain and turning everything around me into a sort of movie that had nothing to do with me. My thoughts regarding my condition, however, were crystal clear.

Following Ella seemed like a nasty idea, but I could have Michael followed. I tried to decide whether there was a moral difference between the two. Of course, if it turned out that Michael had nothing to do with her, then following him would not constitute an invasion of her privacy. I would have to make do with that as an excuse, since I had absolutely no doubt that I had to find out what was going on here, or I would lose my mind.

I was thirty, the same as Michael. We had gone to high school together. I had been to his wedding six years before. I never expected him to get married so young, but since then we had each gone our own way more or less. It was such a strange feeling to sit in this bar and plan in a very technical and structured way how to get the information that might destroy my current life. After I left the bar, I made a few calls from my car and got the name and number of a detective. We met that afternoon and he told me to be in touch with him by the end of the week. It was a Sunday.

I got home before Ella, but discovered it was quite a different place from what I remembered it to be. From the moment I set foot in my house, I felt this urgent need to run away; every corner of the house was under suspicion. Could Michael and my lovely wife have fucked on the bed that I naïvely believed to be mine? Maybe they made love in the bathroom; maybe she put her hands on the sink while he fucked her from behind so they could both see her excited face in the mirror where I shaved every morning. My whole face twisted in disgust as I imagined this scene. I knew that I needed something strong, because the numb feeling had started to take the shape of a real heartache and a stomachache as well. I opened our bar, which turned out to contain a rather disappointing selection. There was one exception though – a fourteen-year-old cognac that her father had brought us from his most recent trip to France.

I'm no big authority where alcohol is concerned and I'm not sure that I could distinguish this French masterpiece from the Israeli variety, which probably tastes like jet fuel, but I guess the mere knowledge that you are drinking quality can make you feel good. I poured a portion unthinkable under normal circumstances, added two ice cubes and sipped – thirty is not too late to develop a healthy addiction to alcohol.

I suddenly remembered the first and only time I got truly drunk ten years before. It was so terrible that I vowed never to repeat it. It happened after breaking up with my second girlfriend, the one who came after Karen, my high-school sweetheart. I was sitting with my friend Peter and two women friends of him. I don't think I actually planned to get myself drunk. I just wanted to escape the pain. My physical condition after my first Long Island gave no indication of what was to follow. I managed to get the right floating sensation and I didn't really participate in their conversation. Most of the time I just observed the reddish fluid slowly diminishing in my tall glass. From time to time, Peter would mention my name and tap me on the shoulder, and everybody expressed their sympathies and I expressed my gratitude and then retreated into my empty thoughts. Still, it made me feel better to be with other people even if I didn't participate in their conversation.

The nasty feeling followed my second Long Island, and it was very sudden. I went to the toilet to throw up and before I managed to get back to our table, I realized that I needed to throw up again. I stumbled outside, collapsed on a chair on the sidewalk and started to vomit ceaselessly. My will power was completely lost. It was nighttime and there was only a thin movement of people in and out of the bar; they all looked at me disgustedly. I looked back at them and felt no shame, only suffering. The earth was shaking angrily in all directions as if it had turned into a huge roller coaster.

After a while, I tried to talk, but all I could utter was incomprehensible moans, since my throat had turned into a pipeline carrying sulfuric acid out of my body.

Later, Peter and the girls carried me home, where I continued to vomit for two more hours. The next day was slightly better, but this certainly went down as my worse experience. Perhaps now I had reached a point in my life that deserved another suicidal act. If Eti had justified that horrific experience, I wondered what sort of chemicals I should try now in Ella's honor. I walked around the house with my cognac in my hand. On one of the shelves by the bookcase, *The Kitchen* by Banana Yoshimoto and the treacherous Italian cookbook lay side by side. Nearby stood a cute glass fish.

"Cheers!" I said, and took another sip.

Ella got me this fish about a month after I met her. It was after my first encounter with her friends. Ella's friends are quite a wild bunch. That evening, I guess I was kind of excited and I didn't speak too much. In retaliation, Ella got me this fish whose mouth seemed open in awe, a hint at my failure to communicate that night. That problem was solved long ago and some of her friends became close friends of mine, but looking at that fish now was rather painful; it seemed to mock me, as if now, five years too late, it turned out that I really was too much of a gefilte fish for Ella.

Ella was the only girl I have ever slept with on a first date. It wasn't long after Michael left to do his Master's degree in the States, and I still had the tendency to measure everything on the Michael scale. Ella was very attractive and I couldn't believe my luck – sleeping with such a beauty on our first meeting. I guess I was so excited about it that it took me some time to realize that I also liked her a lot. I remember thinking that here was my first ever one-night stand, and how unjust it was that Michael probably had thousands of them. It wasn't my looks that prevented me from casual sex; I could only get serious girlfriends.

Someone else with the same looks and a different personality would probably sleep around constantly. Whenever I realized that someone attractive wanted to sleep with me but didn't make me want to marry her, I would explain to her in detailed clarity that she would never ever have a chance with me – that way no one could claim that had I misled her. No wonder they never stayed. I never quite realized that girls also wanted to be deceived sometimes. Years later, Ella and I used to laugh about my having to marry my only one-night stand, thus erasing it from my sexual résumé, since no one can claim to have had a one-night stand with his wife.

In retrospect, our sleeping together on our first date was no surprise. Ella was the wildest woman I had ever laid hands on and I was extremely pleased with myself for having gotten such a prize. All my previous girlfriends, including the mythological karen, were somewhat tame. I had always thought that I needed someone cooler as a counterbalance to my being such a complete nerd. Now it was time to pay the price. At six thirty p.m., Ella got home. I was quite drunk, and that helped me deal with her. I heard the elevator door opening and I got up from the sofa with a stupid drunken smile on my face to greet my beloved wife. I'm not sure why – suddenly the biblical story of Jephthah popped into my head. Jephthah vowed to sacrifice the first one to welcome him home should the Lord grant him a victory over the enemy. Alas, it was his daughter. What a jerk! Did he really think it would be a sheep or an ox? Ella opened the door and I wrapped her in my arms and gave her a big kiss on her mouth. She was quite disgusted.

"Hard day at work?" I'm not sure how I managed to get through that evening. The minute she walked inside, I knew that I would have to get away as soon as possible until Thursday, the day I expected the results of the medical test – was there a malignant tumor in my marriage? I guess the mere decision to disappear the next day made it easy for me to be around her that evening. I wanted to know right away, but I had to wait. I walked around the house planning my moves. I needed an immediate leave of absence from the office for a few days and I needed Ella's cooperation for that – how ironic! Ella sat by the TV and quite predictably noticed my strange mood very quickly. She sneaked up behind me and wrapped her hands around my waist.

"Honey, is everything OK? You're very weird today."

It's funny – in spite of everything, her hugging me was very comforting; it felt like a reassurance that things were still OK between us.

"I'm just a little tired. I'm tired of my work. I need a little time off, by myself. Just a few days." It's lucky that this conversation took place with her eyes staring at my neck. On the other hand, she had her own reasons for not insisting on an eye to eye position.

"Are you sure it's just work you're tired of?"

"Yeah. I don't know, I just need a few days, OK? It's not that there's something wrong between us; I just need to recharge my batteries and think a little bit." It's interesting that the more I continued this sentence, the more I advanced from concealing the truth to active deceit. The next day I called my office and told them I was terribly sick. Ella would tell them that I was sleeping whenever they called and then call me so that I could return the call. When we parted the next day, I felt like I was going for a lifetime. We hugged and kissed and I felt so close to her that I wanted to cry.

"Honey, you're just going for a few days, right?"

"Yeah, but I'll miss you terribly." I started to regret the whole thing and I wasn't even sure that I wanted to hear from the detective.

We could go on like this, couldn't we? But I withstood temptation and left our home with red eyes and feeling like I had no idea what I wanted. I was completely lost. I spent the next three days in a little guest-house in Hararit, a small village of meditators in the lower Ronlee with a beautiful view of the valley of Bet Netofa. To my surprise, I managed to enjoy myself. It was so soothing and I dreaded Thursday so much that I relished every moment of tranquility. I took a little trip to a church carved into a rock not far from the village, I had great meals every day, and only on Wednesday night did I become really nervous and barely got any sleep. The next day I ate the good breakfast they provided in the guest-house – black bread with pine nuts, fine goat cheese and a lot of salad and scrambled eggs. I had three cups of black coffee to make sure I wouldn't fall asleep driving, and then I set out for the land of grief.

"This apartment they go to – it's a kind of a love nest where he meets all his lovers."

"How many does he have?"

"Well, it's a bit banal…"

"One for each day of the week?"

"Yeah, from Sunday to Thursday. He's free on the weekends. He has a wife and a kid."

"A kid? How old is he?" It was amazing how much we'd grown apart, Michael and me.

"Four years old."

"And his wife suspects nothing?"

"I don't know. We only followed him around the apartment, as you requested, that and some general information. I don't have a clue about his relationship with his wife."

"Do you have any idea how long this has been going on?"

"He appears to have rented this apartment for a few years now, but that doesn't really say anything about your wife, does it?"

"I hope not." What difference does it make, anyway? I tried to figure it out. She had been going to that "Italian cooking" thing for a couple of months now. What happened before that? God knows, maybe they switched days. Suddenly, I had an idea.

"Do you have pictures of the other women? I just want to see their faces, yeah? This is not about peeping."

"What is it about, then?"

"I don't know; it suddenly struck me that maybe I know some of them." The fatigue from my sleepless night and the driving that followed had dulled my senses and I wasn't sure why I really wanted to see those other women. I guess I tried to look at this as a sort of a detective riddle to be solved rather than as a personal catastrophe. He rummaged through a bunch of pictures and finally took out four more pictures.

"This is Mrs. Sunday. A pretty woman." The picture wasn't very clear. It was of a fair-skinned lady with shoulder-length blonde hair photographed through a window. It took me some time to realize that I was looking at Lisa, whom he used to date in high school.

"You know her, huh? Sorry, I didn't mean to ruin your day."

"Ruin my day? I think I got the whole decade screwed up."

"What is she to you?"

"Just someone I went to school with. I hope we aren't going to see my mother in the next picture." I tried to speak nonchalantly, but I was way too uptight and that's how it came out.

"No, your mother is probably past her prime, right? This one goes strictly for young, beautiful women. There's Monday." I didn't recognize Monday, but Tuesday caught me by surprise.

It was my wife's dear friend Ruth. This was a global conspiracy; how could it be? I liked Ruth and we had even met for a cup of coffee without my wife on a few occasions. The four of us, Ella, me, Ruth and her husband had had countless dinners together, but not any more, I guess. When I got home, I was delighted to see that Ella wasn't there yet. I opened the bar and it appeared that I had finished what was left of the cognac on Sunday. I took out the vodka, poured a third of a glass and filled the rest with orange juice. She came home at seven p.m.

"Hi honey, I missed you terribly." She hugged me and, as I hugged her back, I realized how much I'd missed her – her smell and those fingers rubbing the hair at the back of my head.

"You've been here for what – ten minutes, and you're already drinking? I'm a little bit worried about you." I'm not very good with games and tactics, so I decided to say what I had to say immediately.

"We need to talk."

"Sure, just give me one minute; I have to go to the bathroom. OK, hon?" When she went out, I told her:

"I'd like to tell you a story."

"Sure, I like stories. What kind of story would you like to tell me?" Such gaiety!

"I'd like to tell you a story about Michael."

"Michael? Who's Michael?" Her answer made me reconsider my moves. This was the moment when she was supposed to start crying, confess her crimes, and tell me that she still loved me.

"Michael is Whoisit." But that seemed to make her angry.

"You really are drinking too much. I'm going to fix us something to eat."

"Wait a second." I wasn't sure what this meant, but I had seen the pictures – not sexual pictures, just her entering the apartment, one kiss, that's all, and it was more than enough.

So I started to tell her about Michael and me.

Maybe later she would decide to cut the crap and talk to me about us. Was there an "us" anymore? Anyway, here's the story of Michael and me:

Michael immigrated from the states to Israel with his family at the age of twelve and we both entered the same secondary school. We were best friends from then on until we graduated six years later when, for some reason, our lives began to take different directions. I guess we never really fitted as best friends. From the minute I met Michael, we had very clear roles in each other's lives: I helped him find his place in Israel. He helped me find my place on the planet Earth. Michael helped me get my first girlfriend when I was seventeen. If it wasn't for him, I'm sure I would have graduated as a miserable virgin; he really did save me. On the other hand, it seemed now that he had given me too much and figured that it was time to take. One spring day, we were sitting in the Bible class playing "Bull's-eye" (a code-breaking game). Bible classes were very liberal events and each student chose a different way to spend this hour. As I was checking the code-breaking data I'd gathered so far, a little note appeared before my eyes. What was written on it caused me such extreme stress that I didn't even try to locate where it came from. It said: *Hi Erik, I love your eyes and the rest of you is also kind of nice. Please get in touch – from the girl who is in love with you.* I stared amazed at this note, which suddenly disappeared. Michael had taken it out of my hand. "Give that back to me!" I gave a scream that was too loud, even for such a liberal event as a Bible class.

"Shut up and cool it, man!" Michael whispered.

I tried to take the note back from him, but Michael has always been quicker and stronger than me.

"Mr. Oz, have you gone mad?" The Bible teacher was obviously right, although after two years of conducting private lessons for the two top students at the front desk, she should hardly complain. The female sex aroused paralyzing horror in me in those days. I did have social relations with girls in my class and I did chat with them like everybody else, but not quite – mine were futile and completely harmless conversations, devoid of anything vaguely resembling teenage flirt. It wasn't that I didn't want more; of course I did. I had lots of fantasies about those girls and what I would do with them. But those fantasies were as remote as possible from the reality of romantic relationships since I had no experience on which to base them. There was a complete cut-off in my brain between the region generating those fantasies and the region responsible for their implementation. Any hint of a remote chance of "dangerous contact" would cause an immediate crash of all vital systems. If I was at a party and a girl looked in my general direction, I would immediately retire to the toilet or move over to the other side of the room, anything to avoid the terrifying possibility of contact.

After class, we had a conversation in the school yard.

"Look, Erik, if you were some ugly creep, I'd probably write you off as a hopeless case. But since you are such a cute guy with pretty eyes, well, don't you think it's kind of a pity?"

"But we don't even know where this came from, 'the girl in love with you'. What is this crap?" I said, trying to find protection from this affliction.

"I noticed that when you were screaming at me in class, Karen was the first to look in your direction, and I've always suspected that she has a crush on you. Anyway, figuring this one out won't be a problem."

"Karen? Are you out of your mind? She's too short! I'm not dating that girl!"

"Too short? Wake up, man! Soon you'll be the only one left in school with no girlfriend. We're no longer ten years old, you know. Karen is very cute and I would gladly bang the shit out of her."

"You would do what to her?" My knowledge of sexual trash talk was somewhat limited, but fortunately Michael thought I was being cynical.

"Anyway, even if you don't like her, you have to start going out with girls, you know? Tell her whatever she wants to hear, that's how you get your way with girls."

Later in life, I learnt that Michael and I had different views about all sorts of things, but back then, he was my mentor and I accepted his pearls of wisdom in a way similar to a Muslim's acceptance of his mufti's fatwa. Later, when Karen and I were together, she told me how Michael explained to her before our date that I was rather shy and that if she wanted me, she should be patient, as it would take me some time to become my charming self around her. Had I known that beforehand, I would probably have tried to end his life in a very painful way.

A few days later, Michael informed me that it was indeed Karen who had sent the note.

"I talked to her..." he started saying and I rudely interrupted him.

"What do you mean, you talked to her? Are you out of your fucking mind?" I screamed pathetically.

It's hard for me to grasp now the kind of paralyzing horror with which girls filled me back then. Michael's tolerance for my ludicrous behavior should be appreciated.

"Erik, get a grip on yourself. It's OK to be a little scared.

I talked to Karen and Lisa, and tomorrow we'll all go to a café and maybe to the movies later. If you don't like it, don't come, but don't scream at me like that, all right?" he said, and left the scene. My first reaction was anger: he can go with both of them to drink coffee and do whatever he wants with them.

But as the day passed, I began to realize that maybe it was worth a try. Nothing would come out of it anyway, I told myself. After the four of us sat down at our table, I became completely tongue-tied. The combination of Karen, who was supposed to be my date, and Lisa, Michael's very good-looking girlfriend, denied me access to my mental faculties. My main concern was where to look when I wasn't staring madly at the menu – I certainly read it with unprecedented thoroughness.

Karen and Lisa were equally embarrassing targets of my gaze, and after a few minutes my eyes, which were shifting frantically from one to the other, became moist and tired. As always in those days, Michael saved the day. He engaged them in casual conversation and as it turned out, he came with some prime intelligence:

"Karen, did you know that Erik is an avid reader and that he wants to be a writer?"

"Really? What are you reading now?"

"I've just finished reading *From Here to Eternity* by James Jones."

"Do you mean James Joyce?"

"Oh God no, I know he's supposed to be the greatest writer ever, but I tried to read *Ulysses* and I couldn't get past page three."

"So tell me, what's so great about this Jones book?"

"Yeah, tell us too!" Michael exclaimed.

"Yeah, tell all of us," Lisa added.

I told them about the suicide of Isaac Nathan Bloom, who thought that being a Jew was the source of all his troubles. Before his final act, he lamented his misfortune in a paragraph where most sentences began with "If only I had done this" and "Why didn't I do that". That was the first time I learned something about myself from reading a book.

I too would waste lots of energy lamenting my mistakes and thinking how great life would have been if only I had done this and that. The experience of reading a novel and drawing conclusions regarding my life seemed terribly profound to me, and besides, this was a great book about World War II, one of my favorite subjects, although it wasn't quite a war novel. Karen seemed to like my answer and we continued to talk about books.

I even began to feel a little guilty because Lisa and Michael were kind of excluded from the conversation. Karen said that she had just read *Horses on the Highway* by Savion Librecht and asked me about Israeli literature. I admitted to not knowing much about it, but I mentioned the Bible, and this crude attempt at humor was received with surprisingly merry laughter.

After we said goodbye to the girls and Michael and I went home together, I engaged for the first time in my life in a boyish trashy conversation about girls: I'll fuck her like this and we'll have a big orgy, the four of us, and I laughed and Michael made a significant contribution to my vocabulary. It's not that I'd never heard those words before; it was the first time I'd actually begun to ponder the meaning of those mysterious words.

A few minutes after Michael and I parted, I was seized by total panic: What should I do the next day in class? How should I behave with Karen? As someone who is involved with her, should I kiss her? Even on that first date I didn't really kiss her. When we said goodbye we stood quite close to each other and my hand was maybe two inches from hers, which caused my heartbeat to accelerate and created electric currents through my hand, almost tempting me to believe that there had been contact, but there hadn't.

The next day I would have to demonstrate my new friendship with Karen, short and imperfect Karen, while Michael and the gorgeous Lisa stood in the corner and made out between classes. The next morning, I was truly terrified. I considered telling my mom I was sick, but this was a lovely spring day and I really didn't want to stay home. Michael and I walked to school together as always, but we didn't say much. I was too tense to talk and Michael did nothing to ease my tension. When I entered our classroom, the first thing I did was to locate Karen. She said hi and smiled and I didn't even manage a response. I moved my head back and forth in an unsuccessful attempt at a polite response and I said, mostly to myself: "Ah, ummmm...." After sitting at our desk, I commenced a thorough reading of the material from the last class – I have never been so prepared for a history class. I didn't talk to her throughout the entire day, and I only spoke a few words to Michael. During the break, I waited for her to leave the classroom before rising from my chair, or if she chose to spend the break in class, I chose a path as far from her as possible. After a few days of such ludicrous behavior, our date seemed to have been forgotten and I could go back to being my good old self, reasonably mobile and chatting with everybody except Karen, of course. My relationship with Michael during those few days was rather cold. I guess he really wrote me off as a lost cause.

The following Sunday, after returning home from another supposedly OK day at school, I was struck by an insight – I guess that was the day I became self-aware. I was already seventeen, I wanted a girlfriend, I wanted Karen and Karen was within reach or at least had been a few days earlier. I needed to do something; calling her was probably a good idea. Actually calling her was a lot more complicated than the idea of calling her. The effort involved dialing three digits and then slamming the phone down in a panic and walking around my room like a delirious prophet, talking to myself. After three hours or ten minutes, I don't know which, I finally managed to dial the whole number. I held the receiver two feet away from my ear as if Karen's voice might fry my brain and I truly hoped she wouldn't answer. She did.

"Hi Karen, how are you?"

"I'm fine, how are you?" The tone was extremely cold.

"I'm also fine." Then, a ten-hour silence.

"Erik?"

"Ahaaaa?"

"Is that why you called me? To ask me how I was?"

"Uhhh... No. I mean, ... No. I guess." Another eternal silence. After an indefinable period of time, I finally managed to utter the following sentence. It came out sort of unclear, as if I were talking with a large piece of apple in my mouth.

"Would you like to meet?"

"To meet?" Her tone changed, I could notice as much even in my catatonic state.

"Do you mean just the two of us? His Highness would actually agree to be seen with me in public? You know that wherever we go, there might be people from school, even from our class. Are you sure you can handle that?" Her tone was very sarcastic, in accordance with the text and with Karen's personality – she was a smart, cynical girl who came to school wearing "All men are bastards" T-shirts. I tried to think how Michael would respond to this offensive, and again I was struck by a recognition that was a million miles away from anything I would have thought of the day before: I am definitely not Michael. Michael would try to impress her with some witty remark or some trick; I was witty only in friendly surroundings and Karen was not friendly at this point. I just had to say what I felt and apologize.

"Erik?"

"Listen, I... I'm sorry... I mean... I know you think I'm a complete jerk after my strange... I mean... behavior in the last few... week. I mean, I know I've been completely stupid, I mean, I'm in shock, you see? I never dated anyone and I sort of don't have a clue what to do. Arrr." (I hope you'll find it in your heart to excuse the somewhat unorthodox grammatical structures I used. I'm actually still quite proud of this speech I managed to utter.) We talked for a few hours on the phone and when I replaced the receiver and my senses resumed functioning normally and even set a new standard of wakefulness, I noticed that the shape of the receiver was practically carved into my hand. A stream of sweat was running down my forehead, and my left hand, on which I had been leaning for the entire conversation, felt as if someone had tried to separate it from my body with a saw. I took a deep breath because I had been inhaling only the minimum required for existence during our conversation.

After that conversation, even before the great date that followed it, marking the beginning of the short path to her being my girlfriend, my relationship with Michael changed. After this huge favor he had done for me, our relationship became more balanced. I became a legitimate citizen of our world. It's not that my position in school had been so bad before. I have always known how to take care of myself. I used to amuse everybody with silly remarks, and I was a pretty good basketball player and a good friend of Michael, a major mover and shaker. Now, I became a respected member of the community by right. I was certainly not the first one to have a girlfriend in our class; most boys had one before me. It was as if I had some hidden depth waiting to be discovered. Now, not only did I have a girlfriend, I became a special consultant in matters of the heart. Girls from other classes came to hear my learned opinion about love.

In a matter of two months, I turned from the kid who didn't understand what everybody was talking about into a women's man.

"So you see?" I told my beloved one.

"Yes. I mean … No." Was it possible that she didn't get it, the bitch?

"Michael is Whoisit."

"Michel is who? Oh, I'm too tired for your nonsense. I'm going up to Betty; I'll be back in an hour and I hope you'll have sobered up by then," she said, and left our apartment. What the fuck was that supposed to mean? Did she think that she could ignore me and continue to have this comfortable and passionless marriage while fucking Michael? What was I to do now? I remembered all the horrible stories of jealous husbands who murdered their wives after discovering they had been unfaithful. I thought that perhaps I had begun to understand them. I too wanted to kill. But what was I thinking – was I becoming a psychopath? What should I do? I was sitting uncomfortably on the edge of my living-room couch, feeling out of place in my own home like someone stuck in a strange city desperate to go home, only I had nowhere to go.

After a few minutes, I realized what I should do. I should go see Michael!

I got his address from the private eye. I went to the posh neighborhood north of Tel Aviv where the son of a bitch had built his villa with money earned in his twenty-million-dollar start-up. I got this information from the Internet having obtained the name of the company from the private eye. I'm not sure which got me more drunk, the vodka or the strange sensation that this was the moment: from now on, nothing would be the same, even though the reason for the change was no big celebration. When I found a parking space not far from Michael's house, it was after eight p.m. Michael was supposed to be at home, having done Ms Thursday. Maybe he had gone back to work.

How can you run a start-up company working eight hours a day? The sign on the house gate said:

"Carrie and Michael Rosenberg". Yeah, that was it: a beautiful house, a little piece of America in Tel Aviv, a red-tiled roof, a broad façade with a colonial arcade in the middle, like the White House. There was a big lawn in front of the house and exquisitely trimmed little trees scattered around. A football lay in a corner; Michael was probably preparing his four-year-old son for the role he had always dreamed of – the quarterback of the Washington Redskins. I contemplated the idea of barging in and accusing him of cheating on his wife in front of his family. The chances of me actually carrying out this daring plan were null, of course, the reason being either my kindness or my being a complete nerd. I took out the mobile phone whose twin brother had gotten me into this mess and dialed Michael's number.

"Helloooo." The very cute voice of a four-year-old. My heart felt a little faint suddenly. That's how I am, a little soft. My thoughts of making a big scene vanished.

"Is your daddy home?"

"Yeah, Dad...." His voice calling his father was so cute.

What an ugly world. In twenty years, with the genes he had inherited, he'd probably be cheating like crazy on his spouse. After a minute or so, I heard Michael's familiar voice and that kind of shocked me. I was swamped with high-school memories. How did my life get messed up like this? After a few hellos he was about to hang up.

"Michael?"

"Who is it? Erik? Hey man! Do you know how many times I wanted to call you? Wow, this is great! Where are you? Here, outside? Come on in!" he continued with enthusiasm that sounded quite authentic, as if we didn't have any issues between us.

"Could you please come out for a minute or two?"

"Why don't you come in for a drink? What's the point of staying outside if you're already here?"

"Michael ..."

"OK, OK, I'll be out in a minute."

A few minutes later, he came out in all his splendor. He hadn't changed much – maybe he'd put on a few kilos. Most people don't change that much between the ages of twenty-four and thirty. He gave me a big warm hug and I tapped him slightly on his back.

"You look great! How long has it been since I last saw you? Shit man! What have you been doing with yourself? From now on, basketball at least once a month, what do you say? So, how are you?"

"Michael, I know. I mean, you and Ella probably decided to drive me crazy pretending you don't know what I'm talking about. Why do you think I'm here?" I half said, half screamed at him.

"What?' I took out one of the pictures showing Michael caressing Ella's cheek in an intimate way that made it hard for me to look at this picture. "That's Ella!'"

"Oh fuck man!"

Michael sat down with his back leaning against the fence, holding the picture in his left hand, covering half his face with his right hand, and repeating the same thing over and over again:

"Oh fuck man!"

I'm not sure why, up until that moment, my pain had been rather dim, not focused. Michael's confirmation of what I already knew made me feel like I had a hole in my stomach, right in the navel. I felt like those apples that look fine and nice on one side but have a big ugly brown hole on the other.

"Will you cut the crap? It's not like you just had a personal disaster, right? I mean, you already knew that you were fucking my wife, so stop acting like a victim!"

Maybe I should have punched him in the face, possibly just as he was coming out of his house, but of course I didn't. It's not that I wanted to do it but refrained; at the critical moment, I never really want to do it.

"You know, I've thought about you many times. I don't know why I didn't call you. It seems as though you at least kept in touch, didn't you?" I burst out laughing; I actually managed to make myself laugh! It really seemed as though it was Michael who had just received the most terrible piece of news. He didn't even smile. We sat in complete silence for a few minutes. There were many things I wanted to ask him, but Michael was the one to break the silence.

"There is one thing I have to tell you. Your wife, Ella – she doesn't know who I am. She really doesn't know that we were such good friends in high school. She doesn't even know my name."

At first I thought that this made perfect sense since she really didn't seem to know who Michael was. Her calling him Whoisit also fitted. Then I started laughing again – it's amazing how liberating a sense of destruction can be.

"What's so funny?"

"I don't know. I mean, am I supposed to feel good about her fucking an anonymous guy? Does that make everything OK now?"

"I'm sorry."

"Well, I hope you are. Could you explain this to me? What is this – is it some new Tel Aviv perversion, anonymous cheating?"

"Sort of."

It turned out that Michael and Ella had met through a website called www.Anonymousinfidelity.co.il. At first they didn't know names and didn't know anything else. Her good friend Ruth had gotten her into it. She met Michael first, and apparently was impressed.

Lisa had nothing to do with the website, of course; they had been high-school sweethearts and lovers for years, long before he got married. This whole arrangement had aspects that would have amused me under different circumstances. All the men in this arrangement were called Samson and the women, Delilah.

"When did you discover that you were fucking my wife?"

When I had phrased this sentence, I hadn't realized how painful it would be to actually say it. I suddenly remembered all my feelings of inferiority with regard to Michael, good-looking Michael, charming Michael, whose dick was bigger than mine. It must have been great for her with Michael if she was willing to risk so much for it. I remembered the stories about Lisa screaming with pleasure during our three-day class trip to the Negev desert. We were all spread over the grounds of the big Ramon crater in our sleeping bags. Luckily I was already with Karen. People who didn't have a girlfriend or who just happened to pass by them by chance (or quite deliberately, perhaps) said that they just couldn't think of anything else. Lisa's moans of delight erased all other information from their brains. I wondered how Ella sounded when she was with Michael. With me, she emitted soft moans and the love declaration that would always follow was also very soft. I bet there was nothing soft about her when she was with Michael – just desperate screams of passion. I wondered if his knowing who she was made it better for them. Maybe it got him excited, the extra sin, maybe it made him try harder, fuck her harder.

"I guess you already know that Ella wasn't the only one."

"Yeah, you already told me that Tuesday Ruth had made the introductions."

"Ruth? I really didn't know that her name was Ruth."

"So, how long did it take you to find out?"

"Erik, you should know that Ella loves you very much. I also love you."

"Well, that's just great."

He waited a little while and then answered my question.

"At some point everybody starts talking about their spouses, no names mentioned, of course. When she started talking about you, there were things that reminded me of you, but I didn't know it was you. Sometimes she would kind of laugh at you: she said that had you met in high school, she wouldn't have even noticed you and you wouldn't have had the guts to even look in her direction. She told me about the only time you got drunk after breaking up with a girlfriend and she thought it was hilarious, the way you were so proud of that one time. And there were all sorts of little details that reminded me of you, your looks and other stuff. But what really made me sure was when she told me about your first date."

"Is there anything she didn't tell you?"

How deep her betrayal was. She had exposed all my weaknesses to someone she believed to be a total stranger. Did she also suspect at some point that Michael wasn't a total stranger?

"Never mind. Go on."

"You told her about a book you read, something by a Japanese author."

"Haruki Murakami."

"That's it! And the book's name was something like a name of a Beatles song."

"*Norwegian Wood.*"

"Yeah! And you told her about a part of the book that really made an impression on you. It reminded me so of our double date with Karen and Lisa, when you told Karen about a book you had read and what it meant for you. In the Japanese book, I think the hero's name was Watanabe."

"That's very impressive."

"And he had this hotshot friend called ... Korasawa, perhaps?"

"No, it was Nagasawa."

"That's it. And when they say their final farewell, Watanabe and his extremely cool friend, he leaves Watanabe with one last moral lesson, but I can't seem to remember what it was."

"He told him never to feel sorry for himself, because people who feel sorry for themselves are the scum of the earth."

"Yeah, that's what it was."

"I guess it applies to me as well, but it's sometimes kind of difficult to follow."

Once a month, on the first day of every month, Mickey arrives at the Dorphman residence to pay his rent. Ms Dorphman, smiling as always, opens the door. They exchange pleasantries and a few remarks about the latest news, and Mickey, six foot four inches of nearly flawless perfection, enters the living room. His shoulders are broad, his limbs are large but not overly bulging, and his hair is brown and beautiful. Elijah is waiting for Mickey in his orthopedic chair and the calculator is ready in his hands. Mickey takes a seat in front of him and greets him politely. Between them is a round mahogany table, and soon Ms Dorphman will serve some tea and one of her excellent pies. Elijah celebrated his thirtieth birthday two months ago. He is four foot tall and his legs are short – short even in proportion to his tiny body. His back is slightly bent, his shoulders are narrow, narrower than those of a child, his neck is eternally inclined to the left, his face is small and triangular with pointed features, his eyes are big and brown. Elijah holds the calculator in his little hands, keys in the dollar rate and multiplies by 500. Between mouthfuls and sips, Elijah and Mickey discuss the level of the municipal taxes, the broken refrigerator and the chances for a revival of the peace process that has faded away. They smile at each other politely, the arguments are fluent and intelligent, and suddenly, the teacup slides out of Elijah's hand and the warm liquid stains his trousers, the chair and the carpet. Ms Dorphman hurries from the kitchen with a dry towel.

"Oh, my dear, you are so clumsy! Those trousers have just come out of the wash. Oh well, when you finish here with Mickey, we shall have to get you a new pair."

Elijah clenches his lips angrily.

"OK, OK, I'm not a little boy anymore!"

But he feels very little and he is swamped with bitterness. Ever since he can remember himself, since the first day he realized how big the trouble was, Elijah has been full of bitterness. Why me? Is this a payment for sins committed in a previous life? Or perhaps I'm being punished for Dad's many infidelities before the divorce? (Hardly likely – why would God inflict a double strike on Mom?) Maybe there's no God and it's all just a random genetic game.

Every time a guest enters the Dorphman residence, he looks at Elijah and exposes his thoughts to him: there is always a little smile of compassion, but mainly, Oh God, thank you for not inflicting this horror on me. Why do I agonize about the promotion denied me, the test I flunked, the costly dental bill for my kids or the hair I'm losing? All those are so insignificant when compared to this horrific existence Elijah has to lead every single day until the last day of his miserable life, this eternal bondage. Yes, Elijah should charge his mother's visitors money; why pay a shrink huge sums of money if one visit to the Dorphman residence can make your troubles seem that much more bearable?

"I think I'll go now, Ms Dorphman. Your cakes are a delight as always. See you, Elijah."

"Yeah, goodbye Mickey," says Elijah, his voice hardly audible as he watches Mickey stepping out of the living room toward the door. After Mickey has left, Elijah turns his orthopedic chair until he faces his folding walker.

He grabs the walker with both hands, stands up, and begins the long journey to the bathroom as he moves the walker forward and follows it ever so slowly.

"Elijah, I'm getting you some new clothes instead of the dirty ones."
"Yeah, yeah, Mother, thank you," says Elijah angrily, and as the words come out of his mouth, he asks himself why is he so angry at his mother, whose devotion is the only thing standing between him and an even more difficult life (if that's at all possible). Elijah enters the bathroom where a pair of small trousers, a little white shirt and a pair of tiny underpants are already waiting for him on a hanger. He takes off his stained shirt and uncovers his tiny whitish upper body. He takes off his trousers and underpants to reveal the tiny penis that has never satisfied a woman and never will unless a miracle occurs, and at the age of thirty years and two months, Elijah already knows that miracles happen only in fairytales. Elijah painfully inspects his defective body in the mirror. He looks at every organ, trying to imagine what it would have looked like had he been normal. Elijah debates with himself: would he want to be someone else? He claims that he would not, he would just want to be an improved Elijah. But on the other hand, if there were a button that would turn him into Mickey, he would surely press it – perhaps with some hesitation, perhaps without.

Ms Dorphman has installed a small bench across the bath so that Elijah can have a bath without slipping and breaking his delicate bones. His short legs prevent him from stepping into the bath, so a tiny staircase with a small railing has been installed as well. Elijah sits on the little bench, adjusts the temperature, and allows himself to enjoy the warmth of the water.

He steps out of the bath, dries himself, and puts on the clean clothes Mother has prepared for him.

He stands in front of the low sink especially installed for him. In the corner there is a small glass containing a small toothbrush and a razor. Elijah rubs his face with shaving foam, places the razor on his neck, and suddenly feels a sharp pain in his finger. He curses: He's cut his thumb, what an idiot, why can't he get anything right? He washes his thumb and wraps some bathroom tissue around it to absorb the blood. Elijah looks in the mirror and notices that there's some blood on his white shirt and he curses again because he knows that blood contains iron, and iron oxidizes and rusts, and that this white shirt is probably doomed. Elijah thinks that it's weird that a stain on a shirt – such a minor problem – can probably never be solved, while the cut on his finger – a tear in a living tissue that's so much more complicated than some silly stain on a shirt – will form a scab in a day or two and then vanish altogether. Elijah goes to sleep. He wraps himself in the blanket, lays his head on the pillow, and within a matter of minutes, he is in another world. He is standing on an infinite white surface. Nearby, thousands of construction workers are laboring, and big trolleys are moving around carrying piles of white bricks. Elijah follows one of the trolleys and finds out that it's headed for a huge canal, a canyon. He approaches one of the workers, a group leader according to the inscription on his back. Elijah stretches his hand up and cautiously taps on the big man's shoulder. He is very nervous, since he has never gotten too much respect from construction workers. The group leader looks at Elijah and turns around; he is obviously excited:

"Sir, this is indeed a big honor! I never dreamed that I would meet the big boss. Wait till the rest of the guys find out you're here."

He shakes Elijah's hand gently and shouts:

"Guys, leave whatever you're doing and come here, the boss is here for a visit!"

The members of the group get off a trolley and one by one, they come to Elijah and shake his hand. Some of them hug him, others burst into tears. The rumor spreads and soon Elijah is surrounded by thousands of workers, all thrilled, all desperate to meet the big boss. Elijah feels kind of awkward; he has never been anybody's boss and he is certainly not big.

"I think there's some misunderstanding here, I mean, I don't think I am who you think I am…"

"It's OK, it's OK," the group leader assures him.

"Everybody here knows exactly who you are. Who do you think we're doing all this for?"

The workers slowly go back to their labor. Elijah, full of curiosity, approaches the edge of the canyon and tries to understand what it is they are building there. The workers carefully unload the bricks, carry them to the bottom of the canyon and lay them with great precision one by one. A huge torn pipe is lying in the canyon and alongside it are big red puddles. The pipe is surrounded by scaffolding loaded with workers. The group leader approaches him again, bursting with pride, and says:

"A few hours ago it was twice as wide and a lot deeper and that conduit was all torn up. I expect we'll be finished here by tomorrow." Elijah feels ashamed; they are all working so hard and they all seem desperately to want some encouragement from him, but he has never had the strength to cheer others on – he doesn't even have enough strength for himself.

"This is really amazing. Can you people handle bigger projects?"

"You can count on us, we can fix it all! Everything here goes back to exactly the way it used to be."

"Exactly the way it used to be? Elijah asks, disappointed. What if I don't want it to be exactly the way it was? You should know that the way things were is sometimes a pretty bad deal. Can you handle that?"

"Maybe, I'm not really sure. I work according to the designs from the planning and design section, I'm sorry."

Elijah feels terrible because the group leader seems upset and Elijah never meant to hurt him.

"It's OK, forget it. Would you happen to know where this planning and design section is?"

The group leader pats Elijah fondly on the head and says:

"I think it's somewhere here."

Elijah says goodbye to the group leader and wakes up. When he opens his eyes, the solution to his problems seems crystal clear. He gets up more energetic than ever before, driven by a surge of optimism. He takes hold of his walker and starts walking twice as fast as usual.

"Good morning, Elijah. What a smile and what a delightful mood, so much energy!" She kisses him on the cheek and he looks at her and says: "Enough complaining, I need to get a hold of myself! What's for breakfast?"

Elijah swallows a huge portion of cornflakes and two slices of bread and, as Mom watches him amazed, he chats quite charmingly and makes witty remarks and he's really funny! Mother can hardly remember the last time Elijah made her laugh – laugh without a strong desire to weep.

"By the way," Elijah says, "you're going to Aunt Sara on Friday, right?"

"Elijah, am I imagining things, or do you actually want to get rid of me for a day or two? Is that why you're in such a good mood?"

Mother is a little bit hurt and a little worried. What is Elijah planning to do while she's away? The problem of satisfying his sexual needs has been a concern for quite a few years. Elijah is a grown man and it seems that as far as his sex drive is concerned, he is as developed as any other male. Mother has tried to broach the subject; she has even considered finding someone who would sleep with Eli for payment – someone trustworthy who wouldn't hurt his feelings or infect him with diseases – but this subject was absolutely taboo and she was never able to talk about it without running into a wall of angry silence.

"No, Mother, whatever makes you think that? You know how much I hate it when you leave me here alone, but... I mean, I know you need some time away from me and don't worry, I'm not planning an orgy for the weekend."

This morning is truly full of surprises. Elijah sees his mother's amazement and quickly lowers his eyes, hoping to prevent further discussion of a topic he is not yet ready to talk about. The days pass by and Elijah prepares himself: he has taken the old saw out of the storeroom and hidden it under the table. He is quite anxious for Mother to leave and he can hardly hide his anticipation: he walks back and forth with his walker like a lion in a cage. In these three days he does more mileage than he's done in thirty years.

The big day is here! Mother makes her last preparations for departure. She packs and asks again and again if there's anything he needs and will he be all right and does he know exactly where the food she prepared for him is and who to call in case of emergency, and he tries to calm her down. Finally, Mother is at the door and she hugs and kisses him and Elijah reminds her that she is only going for two days and it's not such a big deal. Mother is out! The door closes behind her and Elijah can hear her footsteps fading away. There is only peace and quiet and Elijah feels a great sense of serenity.

It's afternoon and Elijah begins the preliminary ceremonies. He prepares a cup of tea, which he drinks with a big slice of Mommy's excellent pecan pie. He watches a movie on cable TV; seated on his orthopedic couch, he is perfectly calm. He takes a shower, shaves, and when night comes, he goes into his room and shuts the door behind him.

Elijah bends down and picks up the saw, lays it on the table, and observes it with deep concentration. Elijah imagines that his feelings at this moment are similar to those of a samurai about to commit seppuku. Those samurai presumably didn't see this act as the end of the road, but rather as the beginning of a new road, since they believed in the transmigration of the soul. Elijah is also about to embark on a new path, but he does not intend to go through the rather problematic stage of death. Elijah will be like a caterpillar that turns into a butterfly.

Elijah brings the chair closer to the desk, holds on to the desk, and lays his head upside-down on it, his hair pressed against it. He has devoted a great deal of thought to this plan, and an inverted head is essential for success in removing his head, otherwise his brains might all spill down through his open neck, and that type of mishap could probably never be rectified. Elijah breathes steadily; he looks at his body with his upside-down eyes, looks at his belly bent against the desk. He holds on to the desk with one hand and takes the saw in the other. Elijah looks at the saw one last time to make sure there is no rust on it, for he would certainly not want his new body to be infected. He places the serrated edge of the saw next to his neck and it tickles him slightly. Elijah takes a deep breath. He is completely calm and confident as he begins to move his hand backwards and forwards. Elijah begins to feel his head becoming slowly separated from his feeble body. His hand is moving swiftly but cautiously, and then he accelerates his movements in order to saw through his spine. No blood is spilt since Elijah's work is very precise.

The saw has nearly cut through; the little piece of skin connecting his head to his body gets cut off, and Elijah sees his little body sliding backwards to the chair. The saw slides from his hand and Elijah (the head) lies face down on the table, thoughts swirling. Elijah is exhausted by the effort.

It's already late at night and he feels his eyes slowly closing. His open neck is defiantly pointing at the ceiling and he expects to wake up with a new and better body attached to him.

Elijah wants to dream again about those thousands of workers laboring ceaselessly to create his new body. He thinks that a special effort will be required since time is short (until Mommy comes back on Sunday) and the present challenge is truly awesome. Instead, he dreams about Odelia, his high-school teacher. The class was about to go on its big annual trip, and Elijah announced, as he always did in such cases, that he wouldn't be able to attend. Odelia said that she and some of the students would gladly push him in the wheelchair so that Elijah could take part in at least some of the activities:

"Remember, Elijah, that all our problems begin with our head and that with a strong will, everything can be overcome."

Elijah thought she had some nerve, that Odelia. He would like to see how she would manage if she had a four foot crippled body.

Elijah also dreams about Rona, the prettiest girl in class. Elijah used to gaze at her with yearning eyes and the only attention he ever got from her was a sympathetic smile and the occasional "good morning."

Elijah opens his eyes and blinks at the sunbeams penetrating the slits in the partly closed shutters. It's morning already. Elijah wants to stretch, but unfortunately, there is nothing to stretch so far. He looks at his body lying on the chair and then begins to notice that something has changed. At first he doesn't quite grasp what it is he is seeing, and then he realizes that his neck (which was sawed away from him) has grown a chin and jaws from which lips are coming out. Elijah's head begins to sweat; this is not going quite according to his plan.

He tries to calm down because he knows that if he shakes his head,
it might capsize and his brains will spill out like jam on the floor.

Nose, eyes and cheeks are growing and it's already known
that this monster's head looks identical to his own.

Elijah doesn't understand this joke, and he begins to cry
for what's the purpose of this game?
Why create another head if it's practically the same?

The process is nearly done, his skull begins to close and his hair is growing long,
when the creation is complete, the monster's eyes begin to glow

the door he opens, he is about to go.

Before he leaves, he looks at Elijah and there is sadness in his eyes,
my father head, for what I've stolen I do apologize

But now, father head, farewell, I wish you all the best
The world is wide, I have to set out on my quest.

The Prophet

"I'm really starting to scare myself, you know?"

"Yeah, honey, you've really been pretty terrifying lately."

Tanya caressed Ethan's cheek and bit his neck.

"I'm serious, don't you see?"

"What is it I don't understand – did another one of your predictions come true?" In the last few weeks, Ethan had surprised Tanya with rather silly accounts of his ability to predict the future. Tanya and Ethan had only been together for six months, six wonderful months. She met him after breaking up with Gal, who had done his B.Sc. and M.Sc. with her in physics and was now doing his Ph.D. When Tanya told him that she was going to take a break from her studies and earn some money, he was totally shocked:

"I don't know – I guess I had higher expectations of you."

Tanya couldn't believe her ears. How infuriating can you get?

They had been together for five years and everybody expected them to get married. Her mother treated Gal as the groom-to-be from the day she met him. Tanya had met him in the first class of the most basic physics course on the first day of the first semester. Tanya was dazzled by his intellect and broad-mindedness, by his phenomenal reading rate that put even a quick and avid reader like her to shame, and also by his looks. Gal was great-looking. He had an aristocratic appearance that suited his occupation and his rather noble origins (as far as it was possible to be of noble origins in Israel), and when they met each other's families, the enthusiasm of parents and relatives on both sides was endless.

Since she was just twenty when they met, her parents didn't press her about getting married. Their confidence in the inevitable outcome was just as strong after five years.

At that point in time, Tanya realized that the problem wasn't her being too young or the need to finish their studies first or any of the other excuses she gave her mother: She just didn't want to marry him and she knew she never would.

Ethan wasn't as good-looking as Gal: his face wasn't as delicately shaped and he had... well, it wasn't a paunch yet, but it would certainly become one if he continued to eat so much – unlike Gal's completely flat stomach, which was toned up during a daily meticulously planned hour at the gym. The first time they slept together, which was on their second date, Tanya was amazed by the intensity of her sensations and the volume of her screams. This was a completely different matter. Ethan truly loved to fuck, he was horny, he bit and squashed her, and after the first round, he didn't go to disinfect himself but rather continued to kiss and lick her. Soon after that, a second time followed and then a third: it was like riding a roller coaster after five years of riding an elevator. And now, for the first time since Ethan and she became a couple, she suddenly missed Gal and his cold rationality. Where the hell did Ethan come up with all this nonsense from?

"Wait till you hear this."

"I'm all ears."

Tanya was very careful not to sound intellectually superior. Ethan knew that she was much smarter and he was very proud of her – but even so, nobody likes to feel like an idiot. Ethan was certainly no fool, but from a strictly analytical point of view, Tanya was definitely on a much higher level.

"Yesterday I dreamed that I was driving a double-decker bus, you know, like they have in London. I don't know why I had such a dream, but it was great."

"Our car is big and green…"

Tanya cheerfully sang the old children's song. She hugged his stomach and bit his back. Ethan turned to face her, kissed her and continued:

"And today, I almost crashed into a bus. I had such a lucky escape – it was unbelievable."

"Define 'almost crashed into a bus' – what happened?"

Tanya was so sure that she would hear a ridiculous supernatural story that she didn't even bother to be shocked by her lover's near miss.

"I was driving along King Saul Boulevard at the Ibn Gvirol junction. I was in the middle lane, the one that continues to The Prophets Street, and the bus made a left, except that he veered so far to the right to be able to make the turn that he almost crashed into me, that jerk. At the last second he moved away from me a little bit. It was so strange. I felt like I was suddenly in control of the bus, moving his steering wheel a little bit so he wouldn't hit me."

"Why didn't you take control of your steering wheel and move a little bit to the right? That seems like the logical solution to the problem, doesn't it?"

"I'm just telling you the way it was, that's all."

"Ahhhh." She sighed.

"Anyway, I'm very happy you escaped that bus."

Tanya hugged Ethan and bit his shoulder.

"I love biting you; you're very tasty."

She drew Ethan to her and pulled up the big blanket that had slid down a little bit.

"Do you remember on Friday, when we were standing in line to buy popcorn at the movies, there was this woman, and you told me that she would buy popcorn and coke, but she actually bought popcorn and water?"

"Yeah, I was pretty close."

"Yeah, but almost everybody buys popcorn at the movies, right?

It seems to me that recently you've become obsessed with making predictions about everything. You cross the street and think that the man standing next to you will probably start walking with his left foot, and then you listen to the radio and try to guess what song will come next, and then you come home and try to guess what floor the elevator will be on. You do that all the time, don't you?"

"I just keep seeing what's gonna happen, what can I do?"

Tanya could feel the resentment in his voice and she knew she had to be careful not to insult him. She sometimes daydreamed about the family they would have together. Ethan, she was sure, would be a wonderful father, and now she was beginning to wonder if she could afford to have such a naïve man as the father of her children.

"No, you don't see what's going to happen. You try to guess what will happen all the time. But you make guesses about things that are very likely to happen, like a lady at the movies buying popcorn, and even then you were wrong because you said she would get a coke.

It's like flipping a coin all day long – half the time you're right and you just forget all the times you're wrong. You see?"

Ethan lay on his back beside her and closed his eyes, and Tanya was quite sure that he didn't understand what she was telling him. He was so convinced of this new mystical ability and it was such a drag! When Tanya first told her mother that she had broken up with Gal, she had responded quite calmly. Mom wasn't stupid and she knew she couldn't make Tanya marry Gal. Her frustration came out on other occasions, when they were chatting while Tanya helped her hang up the laundry or wash the dishes. Once her mother lost control and told Tanya that this was the biggest mistake she would ever make. Tanya didn't really care because she was completely sure that Gal wasn't the right man for her.

Two months ago, Tanya decided it was time to introduce Ethan to her family. She had a serious debate with herself about how to describe Ethan's occupation: Ethan was a carpenter; he designed and built kitchens and tables for people. He was a very creative man and he sculptured in wood and clay. She consulted him. "Maybe I'll tell Mom and Dad that you're an interior designer."

"For God's sake, Tanya, will you stop behaving like a yuppie cliché? Just tell your parents that I'm a very proud carpenter. Maybe before we have this dinner you're so nervous about you should invite your mother over to see all the stuff I've built here – maybe that'll soften the blow!"

That single sentence embodied so much of what Tanya loved about him. Most men wouldn't handle her terror of this meeting so practically. He understood her perfectly and had common sense that worked. Tanya gave her mother the grand tour of the house and Mom was truly impressed. Her friends also really liked him, but suddenly the next planned meeting became a stressful event: Would Ethan share his new prophetic abilities with them too? That could be truly unbearable.

The following day Tanya worked late. She called Ethan and told him she'd be back by ten, but she got home after eleven. Ethan wasn't at home and Tanya thought that he'd probably taken himself out for a walk: Ethan liked to walk the streets of Tel Aviv at night; they weren't long walks – usually not more than an hour. Tanya sank into the couch and stared at the TV. Gal used to reprimand her for this tendency to veg out after a hard day's work. He was probably right, such a waste of living time. Still, after a day of meetings and calculations, she just was too tired to read and just wanted to relax. Ethan didn't have a problem with that; he hardly read at all.

After midnight Tanya began to worry. It wasn't like Ethan to disappear on her like that.

The one thing Ethan and Gal had in common was reliability. Tanya could never live with someone who'd disappear from time to time and then come home telling her fairytales. Relationships are hard enough without having to deal with that shit. She had no problem with him going out with his friends for a men's night – she just wanted to be informed. But now it was very late and Ethan hadn't told her anything. She tried his mobile; he didn't answer. She watched CNN and thought that this had better not turn into a habit or they wouldn't last as a couple. Tanya went to the kitchen to grab something to eat. She used to have these waves of hunger before going to sleep followed by uncontrollable eating. As she took an orange and began pealing it, a folded sheet of paper lying on the desk caught her eye. Tanya noticed that sometimes, immediately after waking up, Ethan would scribble some notes even before washing his face. Then he would fold the paper and put it in a drawer that was filled with a mess of folded papers. Ethan confirmed her suspicion that he was writing down his dreams before they disappeared from his memory. He told her some of his dreams, but refused to show her what he'd written:

"I'm allowed to have someplace that's just mine, aren't I?" Tanya didn't argue with that.

Sometimes he amused her with his dreams, which were as imaginative as the figures he made from wood and clay. But she was mad at him and she thought: Let's see the fool's latest dream. Then she reproached herself, more for attributing stupidity to him than for invading his privacy. She had told herself so many times that she wouldn't let anybody convince her to give up this happiness just because Ethan wasn't a candidate for the presidency of the Weizmann Institute. She handled the sheet of paper with great care as if it were a delicate *objet d'art*, unfolded it and began to read:

I have a problem. Maybe I knew what the problem was in my dream, maybe not, but it's very clear from the depressing atmosphere that I'm in bad shape. I'm alone in the apartment, but instead of a floor I'm standing in some kind of sickly yellow fog. I'm scared. I call Mark and ask him to meet me. It's midnight already and I feel kind of weird calling him so late because of Mira and the kids. I call him anyway, I don't remember the conversation, but soon after that I meet him. I'm not sure where we are, it's like a big round plaza, maybe the State Plaza, only instead of buildings there are some sort of pointed cliffs all around. I tell him that I need a dictionary in order to translate some document. Looking back, I understand that I wanted him to explain my situation to me. Mark doesn't give me the dictionary. Instead, he takes the document and tears it into pieces. End of dream. I woke up feeling very bad, I'm not sure why; have to think about it.

Tanya read the dream twice and thought that she should call Mark, Ethan's best friend since the beginning of time. She hoped she wouldn't wake the baby, but she had to call him. If Ethan wasn't there, she would have to apologize and grovel some.

Mark answered after two rings.

"Hi Mark."

"Hi, how are you?"

"Look, I really apologize for calling so late…"

"It's OK, Ethan's here and there's no problem." For some reason, Tanya was quite sure that there was a problem.

"I'd like to talk to him." Tanya noticed that she was whispering and she cleared her throat to regain her usual level of speech.

"Just a second." Mark disappeared for at least two minutes, which seemed more like twenty minutes to Tanya.

"Listen, Ethan will be home in about an hour, OK?"

It was definitely not OK, but there was no point arguing with Mark. Tanya's mood, which was already pretty shaky to start with, became really bad. He didn't even want to talk to her. Did he want to break up? Maybe she should have stayed with Gal. No, bad moods were a good reminder of Gal's shortcomings. Cheering her up and hugging her for comfort weren't among his fortés. During the first year of their M.Sc., they took an advanced course in quantum theory together. On the day of the exam, Tanya was sick and her results were accordingly low. She got 75 (out of 100) – not a catastrophe, but nothing like her usual performance, and it made her doubt her most important asset – her brain. When she told Gal about it, she expected some love and support. True, this wasn't a disaster on a cosmic scale, but so what? She felt bad about herself and she wanted her one and only to tell her how wonderful she was. Gal was quite devastated by her low grade. He gave her a symbolic hug, but most of all he was anxious to see her retake the exam. He couldn't stop talking about her going out too much and not studying enough and the subjects she should study harder. Tanya retook the exam and got 100 and they went out to celebrate, but that was the beginning of the end for them, even though she needed more time to realize it.

At two a.m., Ethan entered the apartment, but he didn't kiss and hug her immediately as he usually did. She was sitting in the living room and he went to the kitchen. Tanya followed him. He stood by the sink with his back to her. She wanted to go to him and hug him, caress him, but she knew he didn't want that.

"We need to talk."

Here it comes. Until now, she had never been dumped. Since she was fifteen, she had always been the one to end her relationships. She sat at the round kitchen table and he sat next to her, leaning his cheek on his hand. He closed his eyes and tried to figure out what to say.

"Yesterday I had a dream." Tanya listened in silence as he told her what she'd already read. She looked at him and nodded occasionally. When he finished he said:

"So you see?"

"See what?" He covered his face in his hands for a minute. Then he looked at her and reached out for her cheek. Tanya caressed his hand. "The dream – it's about us and about what happened with Mark today.

The yellow fog, that's our disease, your inability to accept me as I am, your looking down on me because you're really so much smarter."

"Ethan, that's not true, I love you."

He continued as if she hadn't said anything.

"And this dream really predicted what happened to me afterwards. I go to Mark and look for a dictionary to interpret a document, that is, I ask him to explain our relationship, and Mark tears up the document, that is, he tells me we're bad for each other…"

"Is that what he told you, to break up with me?" She should kill the son of a bitch!

"No, he didn't, but that's the conclusion I reached after talking to him."

"So you think the dream predicted all that?"

"Yes! Don't you see?"

"But Ethan, you decided to talk to Mark after the dream, right? So the dream didn't predict it, it caused it, don't you see the difference?"

She immediately regretted these words; once again she sounded patronizing. "When I decided to go see Mark, it wasn't because of the dream, but when I got there, I understood that we had to talk about it. So the dream wasn't the reason I went to see Mark, but it predicted our conversation, and what are you going to say now? That I'm flipping coins all day again?"

It seemed that at least he had listened to her during their last conversation. "No, now it's worse. Now you flip a coin, see the result and then search for it, like with the bus. You dreamed about a bus, so you waited for some incident that involved a bus and *voilà*! Another prophecy comes true! Tell me, is it really so easy to convince you that you're an oracle? You know what that reminds me of? In my second semester I had a physics tutor who tried to convince me that I was the next Einstein: 'How brilliant you are, how original, it's people like you the future of Israeli science depends on.' He was talking about some basic first-year exercise I'd handed in, but this jerk of a tutor wanted to fuck me and he would have given me the Nobel Prize to get there. Luckily, I wasn't convinced."

"Look, you *are* the next Einstein or whatever and you're just too smart for me. You should find someone smarter."

Perhaps she really should. Her sweetheart was breaking up with her and instead of talking about love, she was explaining the theory of probability to him. If he wanted to leave her because a dream told him to, what else would his dreams order him to do? Half the world had assumed a faith whose only principle stated that there's lots of magic in the air and that you don't have to explain anything, and she hated it. Maybe she really was a lot more like Gal than she would like to admit. Gal was a cold man and he was terrible in bed, but at least he was on her side in the fight against the spiritual forces of evil. Wasn't it obvious that her idiotic lover could control a bus with the power of thought and prevent an accident? She certainly couldn't prove otherwise.

Tanya watched Ethan, who was sitting on his side of the table without looking at her. He was in another world and she felt very lonely.

A dream match, (or the man who had an extraordinary passion for trains)

Almost every morning, except when he felt too lazy, Rani went to the gym and spent thirty minutes running on the treadmill. He had discovered that time passed much faster when he daydreamed about something. The topic of his favorite fantasy was the yet-to-be-built Tel Aviv subway. (The Tel Aviv subway has enjoyed this status for about 40 years so far.)

"Milan Square!" announces a soft female voice on the Ibn Gvirol line. The train gently slides by the platform. The doors open silently, a few good-looking women board the train, a few others alight, and Rani remains in his place, arms stretched upward to grasp the railing and a foolish smile on his face. He isn't going anywhere – he's here for the hell of it. After a few more stations, the soothing voice announces:

"The next station is Allenby. Change here for the red line!" Rani hurries to catch the red train. That's what he does for the entire 30 minutes – rides from station to station and changes lines.

He tried some less embarrassing fantasies, more suitable- sexual fantasies.

He tried to run while fantasizing that he was fucking Daphnie, a very attractive girl he met at work meetings from time to time. When that didn't work, he would fantasize about fucking her in one of the train cars, concentrating on the plot he had devised:

He boards the train and by pure chance Daphnie is in the same car. At one of the stations, they find themselves alone on the train. [The fantasy takes place late at night in order for it to be credible.] *He approaches her, says hi, and* he cannot ignore her crazy passionate look that tells him – fuck me now! *He undresses her* almost violently *and fucks her from behind as they both stand and clutch the railing.*

Unfortunately, this fantasy didn't accomplish its objective: instead of making his running session easier, it messed up his breathing. The problem wasn't a matter of too much sexual excitement, but rather the opposite. At some point in time, Rani would always get mad at Daphnie for disturbing his joyride. Finally, to his great embarrassment, he had to surrender to the dictates of his body and mind and return to the pure train-ride fantasy that transformed the exhausting training session into an enjoyable pastime - He would be completely unaware of the time passing.

Sometimes after work, Rani would drive to the Azrieli Center, go up to the garden on the roof of the shopping mall, and spend hours watching the trains pass through the Shalom station. He was familiar with all the models: there were single-decker trains and double-decker trains; there were trains with a separate locomotive and trains that had a little engine in every car. He could even identify specific arrays of trains by their numbers and was delighted to see locomotive #754 back on track after a two-month absence for repairs.

Rani was keen to find a girl with whom he could share his passion for infrastructure. Trains were definitely his favorite field of interest, but highway development was not far behind. In addition, Rani was well acquainted with all of the Tel Aviv skyscrapers including those that were under construction and even the ones still awaiting approval.

His subway trains would always speed across a future Tel Aviv where all the prospective skyscrapers already stood firm on the ground, illuminating the Tel Aviv night in a riot of colors.

Rani was a pleasant, attractive guy. He was listed in an Internet dating site and he slept with some of the girls he met there. The problem was that those relationships never lasted more than a month. One month was all most girls needed to reach the conclusion that Rani was the most boring human being on the face of the planet, and they left him. Since Rani really was a nice guy and they didn't want to hurt him, none of them told him the real reason for leaving him, but he understood. Of course, sometimes it was a very convenient arrangement, but when girls he truly wanted were involved, it was very painful.

Daphnie met Nathan (known as Nate) in the swimming pool. She would go to the Tel Aviv university pool twice a week and she was an excellent swimmer . She always swam in the fast lanes, where she was faster than all but the best male swimmers. She derived a kind of sadistic pleasure from swimming behind a slower male swimmer: she would tailgate him and then overtake him and cut him off quite brutally as she returned to her lane. The bigger and stronger the man, the greater the pleasure – she immensely enjoyed teaching those chauvinist pigs a lesson. Nate was one of her unfortunate victims. After swimming for about thirty minutes, during which Daphnie passed him mercilessly at least five times, they reached the side of the pool at the same time and rested for a while.

"Well, aren't you gonna kick me in the face? Go ahead, I love feeling your elbow jabbing me in the side," he said, smiling broadly.

"I really don't know what you're talking about." Nate stuck out his tongue in response to this protest of innocence and Daphnie couldn't help smiling. In spite of his inferior swimming capabilities, Nate was a tall, good-looking charmer, and on top of it all, he seemed like a nice enough person. He asked her if she would be interested in teaching him how to swim freestyle. Daphnie declined, not possessing the patience required of a teacher, but she did give him her phone number.

The following evening, Nate took her out to one of Tel Aviv's most expensive restaurants. He picked her up in his brand-new Alfa Romeo. A soft jazz theme murmured through the superb sound system of his car, but Nate told her that if she preferred to listen to Britney Spears, he would have no problem with that. Jazz had never been her favorite type of music, but somehow it seemed particularly suitable to the exclusive atmosphere in this car. Nate's outfit was elegant without being pretentious. He exuded a wonderful odor – Daphnie couldn't identify the perfume, but she was quite sure that it was far too expensive for any of her previous boyfriends and lovers. They were greeted by a pleasant and elegant-looking waiter whose stiff demeanor seemed rather Prussian. "Good evening, sir. I have prepared your usual table. Will that do?" "Sure, that's great, but you should really stop with this 'sir' business, Victor."

"Most certainly, sir." Victor the waiter led them to their table where a champagne bottle set in a bucket of ice was already waiting for them. They started with a litchi Margarita that didn't get Daphnie drunk, but made her feel even better than she had to begin with. For the first course they had crab bisque that was so exquisite it almost brought tears to Daphnie's eyes. Occasionally Nate would lightly caress her hand and fingers with his large hand. When they had finished their soup (leaving not a single drop in either bowl), he kissed the back of her hand:

"I hope you'll excuse my Polish manners. It's just that I really wanted to kiss you." For the main course they had lobsters, and his deft assistance in dismantling the monster provided plenty of opportunities for gentle and exciting touches. For dessert they had a delicious *tarte aux poires*. The pastry was crisp and sweet and the pears were dripping with syrup. When Nate ordered port after they had already consumed a bottle of wine and a bottle of champagne, Daphnie remarked with rather a silly smile on her face:

"You're trying to get me drunk, aren't you, so you'll be able to carry out your wicked plans!"

"Definitely!" he replied, and indeed he did.

They drove to his luxurious apartment in one of the most beautifully renovated condos on Shabazy Street. Nate proved himself to be a magnificent lover. He was powerful but tender, and after three orgasms that left her completely satisfied if a little exhausted, Daphnie snuggled up to his big body. He enveloped her in his big arms and continued to kiss her gently until she fell asleep. Daphnie couldn't believe her luck. Now she needed to work out how not to lose this perfect man who could hardly swim.

Then, having fallen into a deep sleep, a hedgehog appeared in her dream. A talking hedgehog.

"Daphnie!"

"Yes, Mister Hedgehog?"

"You're very pleased with yourself, aren't you?"

"I sure am! Would you believe it? Accidentally running into such a treasure of a man in the swimming pool?"

"Daphnie, the man who's holding you in his arms will cause you nothing but misery!

You must leave this apartment first thing tomorrow morning and never return here again, ever!"

"Are you out of your fucking mind? Leave me alone, hedgehog!"

Mister Hedgehog arched his back, his quills pointing at her like spears in an ancient Greek military array, and he snorted at her grumpily: "If you meet this man once more, you'll marry him and there will be no end to the suffering this perfection of a man will inflict on you. During the first year, everything will be fine and you'll become pregnant. Your troubles will begin after you give birth to his child. He will start cheating on you constantly. Nate isn't such a bad guy; his intentions are actually quite honorable. It's just that he's such an attractive man that temptation crosses his path on a daily basis. Wherever he goes – work, the pool, when he simply walks the streets – women stare at him, say inane things to try to make conversation, and it takes no more than his decision to turn these gentle hints into dates, affairs, or one-night stands. During the first eighteen months following the wedding, he will make a real effort to restrain himself. But after the first infidelity, a slew of infidelities will follow. Obviously, it won't take you long to realize this, but he'll beg your forgiveness and promise to be faithful. And for a while he will. You will believe that at long last you have achieved peace of mind and happiness. But two years later, following the birth of your second child, there'll be trouble again. This time, you'll suffer from post-natal depression that you won't be able to handle. Your career will collapse and soon afterwards you will, too. When you separate, you'll be in such a precarious mental state that you'll no longer be able to fulfill your maternal duties. Leaving your children with Nate will be the last straw, completely shattering your self-esteem, and you will be committed to a mental institution.

After a year of hospitalization, your condition will improve and you'll return to society. You'll get to see your kids once a week, but they'll already have a new mother, Nate's new wife, a very confident woman – like you are now – who'll win their hearts, and their longing for her while they're with you will cause you great pain. You will never regain your present level of confidence and strength. You will lead a bearable but a truly sad existence until the day you die."

"How do you know everything you've just told me?" Daphnie asked apprehensively. She didn't really believe this nonsense, but his vision of her future was so horrifying that she couldn't avoid worrying that some of it might be true.

"The source of this knowledge I cannot reveal, but I can prove the truth of it. I predict that tomorrow morning, the first pair of eyes to look at you will not be Nate's."

"What eyes? Will my mother drop by for a visit or what? What the hell are you talking about?"

"Be quiet, you rude woman! Tomorrow you will see for yourself!"

Mister Hedgehog snorted, sneezed and disappeared.

Daphnie woke up and smiled. She stretched her hand toward the other side of bed and, failing to touch anything, opened her eyes. Could Nate have abandoned her in the middle of the night? That was impossible, seeing that she was sleeping at his place. The time was ten past nine in the morning. She yawned, wrapped herself up in the big quilt and closed her eyes. The next time she woke up, she felt a slight tickling sensation on her neck followed by a mischievous hand delightfully caressing her tummy. She sighed, felt a kiss on her lips, and heard Nate whispering in her ear:

"Good morning, darling. Don't open your eyes... wait a second, don't open them, wait... Now you can open them!"

Daphnie opened her eyes and saw a breakfast tray standing in front of her. On it was a toasted sweet roll cut in half flanked by three tiny bowls containing apricot and strawberry preserves and a small ball of butter. There was also a glass of fresh orange juice and, on a bigger plate, a finely cut Arab salad, a slice of avocado, a chunk of fine ripe Camembert cheese and two fried eggs that resembled a pair of eyes staring at her. Looking at those eggs, Daphnie knew that they reminded her of something, but she wasn't quite sure what. The eggs were shaped like a heart; how romantic! The yolks were positioned in the middle of the two halves like earrings in earlobes, and the salad and avocado and camembert were arranged around the two white hemispheres like curly hair spilling over a forehead or... Daphnie suddenly noticed that the pointed end of the heart-shaped eggs looked like a pointed nose and the food around the eggs... well, it looked like a hedgehog! She laughed at the association and cut herself a piece of camembert. After taking a big bite, she looked at the plate again, and for a split second, she was almost sure that she saw a real hedgehog looking at her from her breakfast plate. She recalled the dream and choked, propelling the delicious cheese right into Nate's amazed face.

"Shhh, careful now, would you like some water?" he said softly, caressing her, but Daphnie hardly heard a word. She was deeply engrossed in somber thoughts about the hedgehog and his horrific prediction should she stay with Nate even one more day. She debated with herself whether this dream was worth her attention, since she was a rational woman and not some superstitious ignorant fool, but she couldn't deny the fear that suddenly gripped her, and she continued to eat her breakfast sadly. At least this Nate had given her a world-class fuck and a great breakfast, she thought. Being a very sensitive type, Nate realized that Daphnie had experienced a sudden and sharp mood swing, but she obviously didn't want to tell him about her nightmare and attributed her sudden bad mood to a severe headache. Nate soon realized that she wasn't going to tell him what was bothering her, so he dropped the subject. After saying their goodbyes, Daphnie went home and tried to spend a lazy Saturday watching DVDs and snacking, but she couldn't stop thinking about Nate and her dream. The more she thought, the more she tended to dismiss the imaginary hedgehog as a pair of fried eggs that differed significantly from a pair of real eyes despite a certain superficial resemblance. She also remembered that just a couple of weeks before, her friend Tanya had been dumped by Ethan, her cute and stupid boyfriend who had been ordered to leave her in a dream. They'd spent hours laughing and ridiculing him and his stupidity, and Tanya told her that even though she was depressed, she considered herself very lucky not to have married this spiritual but unstable guy.

By the evening, Daphnie managed to convince herself that Mister Hedgehog was a figment of her imagination, and she called Nate to apologize and ask whether he wanted to get together again. Not surprisingly, he did. Alas, Mister Hedgehog made his second appearance the following night and told her that it was indeed he who had been looking at her out of the heart-shaped eggs. He added that denying the truth would not do her any good. She must realize that he was as real as she was, he said, and he made another prediction: the next day, a work colleague whom she considered cute but rather boring would ask her out.

If she could overlook his tendency to pontificate on the plans of the National Railway Authority and the potential advantages of electrifying the system in spite of the rather high initial cost, this man would make her a spectacularly happy woman with three fine healthy children, a pleasant house in the suburbs, two dogs and a cat. Mister Hedgehog, who seemed to be afflicted with a chronic cold, sneezed again before disappearing.

The next day, just as Mister Hedgehog had predicted, Rani made his move and asked Daphnie out for a cup of coffee. Because Rani worked in a high-tech company and Daphnie worked for a venture capital fund which invested in that company, they had met a few times at meetings. Rani had noticed Daphnie long before. Not only was she a beautiful, charming woman, but her summations regarding his company's potential markets and the risks and opportunities involved were quite brilliant. Rani hoped that he had finally found a girl who shared his interests. When Rani approached her, Daphnie was a bit surprised, and she immediately remembered Mister Hedgehog's prediction. She appraised Rani, who was not at all bad-looking and smelled quite pleasant as well, and decided to give him a chance. Rani couldn't believe his luck: Daphnie was bright, attractive and amazingly cool; she had everything a guy could desire except for a genuine interest in mass rapid transit systems. She had grown up in Jerusalem and, although she had moved to Tel Aviv, was still a staunch Jerusalemite. Rani had a great idea: instead of the standard "cup-of-coffee" date, he would show her that even though Tel Aviv wasn't blessed with quaint streets like the ones in Jerusalem's German Colony, it had other things going for it. He would take her to the cliff near the Hilton Hotel to watch the sun set over the Mediterranean!

He had already planned the amusing anecdotes he would tell her. At age fifteen, when he first stood at the edge of the cliff, Rani was astonished to discover how curved the horizon was. It was the first time he comprehended that he really was living on the surface of a sphere. He used to amuse his friends by saying that he might publish this discovery in a scientific article, assuming that nobody had done so beforehand! The following Friday afternoon at four o'clock, he parked his car near the Opera Tower as planned, and he and Daphnie set out on a leisurely one-hour stroll along the promenade by the sea toward the cliff. The date began on a positive note: there was a refreshing breeze and pleasant afternoon sunshine – a typical autumn day. It turned out that Rani's interest in and profound observations of the Tel Aviv skyscrapers had produced some pretty imaginative images, which he shared with Daphnie. When they passed by the Isrotel Tower, he told her that he wasn't sure whether the tower resembled a half-eaten corncob or a huge can of air freshener for the bathroom. Daphnie thought that perhaps Mister Hedgehog was right and this Rani fellah wasn't so bad after all. Just a few minutes before five, when the sun was due to set, they passed the Hilton and started to make their way up the short trail leading to the top of the cliff near Independence Park. At 4:55, they jumped over the low fence and sat on one of the rocks at the edge of the cliff. The horizon spread before them like the rim of a huge inverted plate. The sun, suspended above it, radiated a swathe of gold that reached the bottom of the cliff. The breakwaters lay beneath them like huge anchors holding the land in place, and among them there were a few miniature people bathing in spite of the autumn chill. Several sailboats cruised far off and a few wind-surfers glided over the surface of the water, wobbling occasionally like butterflies trying to maintain their equilibrium. How tragic it was that despite the beauty surrounding them, the first thing to catch Rani's eye as the sun was setting in orange and purple was the hideous Reading power station, belching a disgusting black cloud into the Tel Aviv sky.

"This is really beautiful; I've never seen such a magnificent sunset."

"Yeah," replied Rani, but the switch in his head had already flicked to the wrong position.

"Did you know that Reading emits twelve tons of ash particles into our atmosphere every twenty-four hours?"

"You can't be serious!" Daphnie exclaimed, but tried to maintain a positive note:

"Never mind, it's so beautiful!"

"Yeah, but it's important to mention it. I wish they'd get on with the plan to move the power station away from the city. Do you know how much the land under this stupid power station is worth?" He went on to describe the immense value of the Dov Airport land nearby and the wonderful real-estate projects that could be erected once the thorn-in-the-flesh airport was evacuated; from there, the discussion about the plan to construct a new airport on an artificial island off the coast of Tel Aviv (a secondary but no less important topic) was really unavoidable. However, when Rani began the completely justified lecture describing the terrible hardships endured by the developers of the new international air terminal, Daphnie informed him that she had a headache and wanted to go home. The forgotten sunset had long since disappeared. The next night, Daphnie shouted furiously at Mister Hedgehog:

"Are you out of your fucking mind? Do you really believe that I could be happy with this wacko? The man is a walking sleeping pill! After listening to him for more than two minutes, I wanted to die! I don't ever want to see him again!"

"Give him a chance, you rude, impatient woman, and you'll see what a gentle, considerate husband he'll be."

"Not in this life I won't."

Mister Hedgehog was mad as hell, but being a sensitive and empathetic hedgehog, he felt sorry for her despite the insult he felt on behalf of his hobby-mate and the volcanic anger he felt toward Nate, the egocentric charmer.

"Oh well, you annoying, superficial woman, you can have Nate if you so desire, but there are conditions. Nate will be unfaithful six times; these will all be relatively insignificant infidelities and he will always love you."

"So I can cheat on him too, right? In retaliation?"

"Do as you wish, you treacherous woman!"

"It's a deal!"

"Do you really prefer this charming philanderer to a faithful and broadminded man such as Rani?"

"Anytime!"

"Oh well…," Mister Hedgehog sighed in desperation. "Could you do me a small favor before we part?"

"But of course, Mister Hedgehog!" Daphnie was so grateful that she would even sleep with him if so requested.

"Could you please wipe my nose? I have a terrible cold and my forelegs are too short to reach my long nose."

Daphnie pressed a handkerchief to his nose and he discharged a noseful of greenish snot, snorting loudly. Mister Hedgehog took a deep breath (his first in a few years), retired to his favorite reading corner where the latest issue of *The Hedgehog Infrastructure Review* awaited him, and read it from cover to cover without missing a single word.

Made in the
USA
Columbia, SC